Forever's Too Long

HELEN KRUMMENACKER

Cover art by Allan Krummenacker

Forever's Too Long

ISBN: 9781096235484

DEDICATION

To Allan Krummenacker, whose enthusiasm for my story helped keep me working at it even when I felt lazy, and whose research on publishing and marketing for the Para-Earth series (our collaboration) has been so helpful in managing the release of this book.

CONTENTS

ACKNOWLEDGMENTS

First, I'd like to acknowledge some of my creative influences. I stand on the shoulders of giants. Raymond Chandler, Marv Wolfman, and Dan Curtis all helped shape modern storytelling in the genres this crosses. Jim Butcher showed me there's a demand for old-fashioned detective stories with supernatural twists.

Next, a nod to friends too many to name who encouraged my delight in words and storytelling. If you think I might mean you, I do. For me, all forms of art are essentially about communication. Unless there is someone to look, to read, to watch, or to hear, the creative work is nothing but meditation.

Finally, those who gave me real, practical help getting this thing ready. Allan Krummenacker who I've worked with on the Para-Earth paranormal/science fiction series, Caroline Henry (the alpha of beta readers and PenWoman extraordinaire), and the other beta readers:

Danarra Ban, author of Suicide Drive and Juror in a Desert Town

Richard Caminti, coauthor with Allan on the upcoming The Pass

And Seanna Watson, Christopher Perez, Sherry Martin, and Vincent Cleaver

PROLOGUE

Clara Thomas was almost finished packing when the phone rang. "Good morning," she said.

"So glad I caught you, Clara. You're being sent to America on a case, aren't you?"

"Sir Lynn! Do you need any errands taken care of while I'm there?" She was being cautious. Lynn Fox was a spymaster, and 'errands' was a good word to use on a hotel phone, where the security of the line might be in question.

There was a chuckle on the other end of the phone. "No need to be so formal. I'm your brother, after all, or married to your sister, which amounts to the same thing. Lynn will do just fine. I just called to give you a little advice. I know Interpol needs to recruit more people. Trying to rebuild such an organization is a major task. Well... they'll have given you some files of people they'd like you to interview as possible options. Somewhere on that list there will be a Major Rafael Jones. Near the top if they've had the sense to prioritize them. I think you should read his file first thing. I think he could be a serious asset."

"To Interpol?"

"To them, yes. Maybe in other ways, as well. He has a great deal of potential. I know one of his godmothers."

"Is that all you're going to tell me?" Potential had room to mean all kind of things. But he'd seen potential in Clara, so she trusted him to be choosing well.

"All I can right now. I'd have to meet him for myself to have a better idea. As far as Interpol goes, he's very fluent in two languages, passable in four more. He has a reputation for getting along with very nearly everyone— he makes friends easily, and given that Interpol is all about local cooperation, you could use that. Law enforcement has been his career and he has already worked with an international team. He's ideal for Interpol's needs."

"But you're also interested in him."

"On a hunch, my dear, but my hunches are usually reliable."

"I'm intrigued. Major Jones, you said."

"Rafael, if there's more than one."

"Shall I call you after I've made contact?"

"That's an excellent idea. I'd like to get your impression of him."

"Until then. Give Susan my love."

"I certainly will, and all of mine, too. Safe travels."

With the call over, Clara went to the window and took a moment to look over the city she was in, Brussels, on the continent. Just a few years ago, it seemed like war was everywhere and nothing was safe. Now she could turn her head and look toward England, her homeland, and know that ships were plying across the waters once more. She was soon boarding an aeroplane for America, one laden with passengers, not combatants or weapons. The world was at peace, but her own heart... she didn't think she'd ever be as lucky as Susan, to find someone who was as real and kind as Sir Lynn Fox. He might be more than a decade older than his wife, but what was that when people were perfect for each other, as they were?

Work was better than love, if you didn't have the right one. It gave you stability, purpose, and things to be interested in. Right now, she was interested in getting the file on Rafael Jones to find out what made him important enough to get Lynn's attention.

A WOMAN FOR A PARTNER

1947 seemed like it was going to be a excellent year, but I'm no vintner. My name is Rafael Jones, and this was the year I was going into business for myself. I felt strongly about it; I'd worked for the government for 17 years, between joining the police and then the Army when the war started. I'd learned a lot doing it, like what I was good at and what I wasn't. I could talk to people, getting inside their heads. Sometimes, I could find a missing person like they'd sent me a postcard. I was good at keeping track of rules, too. I just had my own way of dealing with them. Some needed to be followed, even if it was inconvenient or even risky, because they protected the public. Others needed to be ignored, for the same reason; missing persons had ended up being my specialty, and I left some cases 'unsolved' if I found out they'd had a good reason to disappear, like an abusive home. So you can see why I wanted to go independent.

I even had a regular business client lined up already, Eugene Marshall who was an investor, inventor, and industrialist in that chronological order. Thanks to him, I hadn't hesitated to lay down the six months advance rent (which included an apartment on the second floor) and insurance. It was my mom, though, who sent me a brass plate for the door: Harmony Investigations. That had raised my client's eyebrows, not that he minded, but he didn't see how the name would work as a sales pitch until I pointed out to him that a background check isn't just to find out if someone has ties to foreign powers, but also if they work well with others. I love a missing person case that ends in a joyful reunion, but I'm not tracking down a battered wife who got away. If I do my job right, I'm going to solve problems, straighten out chaos, and bring people's lives back into harmony. For some reason, I didn't tell him that the main reason I came up with that name is because music is my first love. It hadn't taken me much longer to discover girls, though.

While I was putting the brass plate on, I noticed there was a faint design etched lightly into the surface. It was odd... there was a shape in each corner, birds or something. They had wings, but I thought one looked more like a bull. I sighed. It had probably gotten placed facing something that still had etching fluid on it and picked up a faint design. It was only visible from the right angle in the right light, so it wasn't really a problem, but if I was going to have a logo I wanted to plan it.

I heard an echoing sigh from behind me. "Excuse me," said a rich contralto voice, "is this the office of Raphael Jones?" Her accent could read for the BBC, and so she got the stresses and vowels on the name just off enough that I heard it spelled the English way in my head.

"Close enough," I said, turning around and switching the screwdriver to my left hand so I could offer her a handshake.

She was worth looking at. She wore a dark blue suit with a cream blouse, very professional. A little cream beret perched on her head looked a bit like a meringue. I suspected she had a sense of humor. Her hair was dark, and so were her eyes, but they had a sparkle to them. I couldn't easily estimate her height because there were a couple of steps up to the brownstone and she leaned forward to shake my hand rather than finish climbing. Well, there wasn't a handrail so I kept her hand and gave a slight lift to it which she read correctly and came up. I smiled. She'd be a good dance partner, I thought briefly, but I still caught her name as she said it. "Clara Thomas, it's a pleasure to meet you. Do you prefer Mr. Jones or Ma—"

"I'm a civilian now," I said a little gruffly. "You can call me Mr. Jones if you like, but I'm usually just Jones or Rafael."

"Rafael," she said it right this time.

"Clara, the pleasure is mine." I said it the way she had, broad vowel on the first syllable, rhyming with car, not care.

"Miss Thomas, I think, Mr. Jones. I'm here on business. I just wanted to make sure I was saying your name right."

I opened the door to my new office. "I'm still getting set up, but come on in and tell me what you need." As she passed me, I thought I caught a hint of sandalwood and violets. Her height, by the way. was just about an inch off from mine with her heels on. She glanced around the room, taking in the second-hand furnishings, the windows not yet washed after the last rain, and the boxes waiting to be unpacked. She casually pushed a chair into place across from the desk.

"Don't be in a rush to unpack," she said. Not exactly the conversation starter I expected, but then I didn't expect someone showing up with my rank at time of discharge on the tip of her tongue. I hadn't even written to my parents about the promotions, not after First Lieutenant. I hadn't seen real combat in the war and the ranks felt like stolen valor, even if it was necessary considering how many people and and cases I was handling in the war crimes aftermath. Yes. I'd had to quit my job with the civilian police in order to join the military because I'd been labeled "essential personnel", only to find myself stuck in military police: enforcement at first and then the CID.

"Let's be frank," I said. "Do you have something I can do for you as a private investigator?"

She hesitated. "Yes."

"You also want something else from me."

"I'm with an organization and I was hoping you might be persuaded to come work for us."

"Not likely."

"You'd travel the world."

"Military recruiters tell everyone that."

"I'm not military, Mr. Jones. I'm Interpol."

"What?" I didn't believe what I was hearing. I thought they were defunct and couldn't imagine how they restarted after Berlin was split.

"We're a new organization. Not the one the Nazis took over. Surely you can see that with greater mobility has come greater opportunities for crime to go international, and therefore police need an international resource to fight back. You've already developed a reputation of being able to work with teammates from multiple countries and organize them based on abilities."

"Assume I'm not signing up. What else can I do for you?"

She switched her pitch pretty smoothly as she explained her current case. "Some pre-Revolutionary Russian art, jewelry, and other valuables have been fenced in this city. We believe a small criminal ring has smuggled out a large cache and want to catch them."

"So Russia can get their treasures back."

"Theoretically that's why we been asked to get involved, but I'm interested mainly because there have been corpses showing up in the same cities that similar artifacts have been sold in before."

"Oh."

"Are you interested?"

"I am. But aren't you more about getting cooperation from the local police?"

"The idiot assigned as our liaison officer thinks it's likely a legitimate collector fallen on hard times and should be a low priority unless we can provide more evidence of wrongdoing."

"Evidence you'd like me to find for you."

"Evidence I'd like you to find *with* me. I'm used to field work myself."

I was getting more interested again. If there were killers loose in the city, getting enough evidence to get the police interested could save lives. Plus, I'd be spending time with Clara Thomas, and I'd always wanted to have a woman for a partner, to be honest. It's just an opinion, but I suspect women, at least the kind of women who would be interested in police work, are going to be more observant, less trigger-happy, and more inclined to the right kind of teamwork, compared to the male of the species. "Fine. Do you have a list of missing items that we can take around to the fences, or...?"

She shook her head. "I'm afraid they didn't disappear from a single source. And the times they disappeared in were not the best for records being kept. However, I studied up on Russian art styles and I think I'll be able to spot items we should be suspicious of."

"Got it. You'll know it when you see it. I have some vague ideas about jeweled eggs and religious figures or birds painted on black backgrounds, but I might do best providing the distraction while you nose around."

"Try showing them a little leg," she joked.

"I don't think Big Ricky over on Main Street's going to fancy that, but it just might work over at Duvall's Estate and Auction House." I opened one box and grabbed a notebook, tossing it to her. "Here's a list of known fences and dealers who are none too particular where goods come from. I presume we can eliminate things like auto shops as irrelevant to your art thieves, but we can figure out how to prioritize the others. Art dealers before low-end pawn shops, that kind of thing."

She started running an eye over the list. "About flirting. I didn't actually mean—"

I held up a hand. "I get it. You're usually the distraction and couldn't resist making the wisecrack you usually hear." I smiled, "It gives me an idea, though."

AN ENCOURAGING SMILE

My car was nicer than my office, bought new a couple of months ago when I came back from Europe. I'd chosen a tan paint job so it wouldn't be too hot in summer if I had to sit in it while on a stake out, and even on a new car tan was boring. Boring is good when you want to go unnoticed. As I held the door open for Clara, she tried again, "You know, if you did come work for Interpol, we'd pay moving costs. That would include shipping the car."

I got into the driver's seat. "If you even want to talk to me about going to work for Interpol again, you'll need to do it while we're on a date."

She frowned. "That's not a deal. I'll only go out with you if I want to go out with you." She couldn't help but look me up and down, though. The possibility of her wanting to was in the air, and I let her think about it while I got the car in gear. Not to sound vain, but I knew my profile wouldn't count against me. The next thing she said was, "Weren't you engaged to a translator working on witness statements?"

"I was. Notice the past tense."

"What happened?"

"No discharge date set yet when a captain whose tour of duty was wrapping up took an interest in her."

"I believe your government has an opinion about war brides who are in it for the green card."

"And I have an opinion about the kind of guy who would turn in a gal he cared about who was still suffering the aftereffects of war trauma and needed to get away from it all."

"She was a civilian."

"Civilians see their share of things, too. I'm not judging." I didn't mind that Clara was judging a little, though. "I swear, if you tell on her, I'll say she dumped me because he was taller and we argued about religion."

Clara laughed. It was short, and throaty, a sort of musical burble. "You really do care about her."

"If I didn't, I shouldn't have asked her to marry me. But I'm not still hung up on her, if that's what you mean, not any more than any other ex." I changed the subject. "Enough about me. You've learned all about whatever is in my file, but all I know about you so far is your name, and that you work for Interpol."

"Yes."

"Come on. Who's your favorite movie star?"

"I don't go to the cinema that much. But... I haven't seen a Cary Grant film I didn't enjoy."

"You've got good taste. I like his comedic roles especially. Favorite food?"

"Does one have such a thing?"

"I like a nice spaghetti and garlic bread, myself."

"Well, I'd say it's awfully fun to get a fish and chips takeaway."

"Where'd you go to school?"

"Someplace dreadful that you've never heard of. Why did you only take one semester of college?"

"My parents were using investments to pay for my college. The market crashed, the business was losing money because dad had to give a lot of customers credit. I didn't want to stretch them any further so I dropped out and got a job."

"I did go somewhere nice for my degree. Oxford. Mathematics."

"With a degree like that, it's a wonder you didn't become a code breaker."

She didn't say anything and didn't stir other than to look at me from the corner of her eye. "Oh,"

I said. "But from that to Interpol?"

"Criminals use codes, too. Besides, that's not all I did. Is that the antiquities dealer we're headed for?"

"Yeah. I just need to find parking. Want me to let you out so it's not obvious we're together?" She did, and I stopped. Wasn't a bad view watching her walk away, and it was probably better to take up the conversation again later anyhow. She was a private person and I didn't want to press her for information too quickly or she'd likely close up. Some things she probably had to be careful about, too, like her work during the war.

When I got to the antique store, I pretended, fairly loudly, to be looking for something for my wife's birthday, with plenty of hints that she was rich and cultured and I had control of the money but no idea of the difference between a Chippendale and Art Nouveau. I looked at some very pretty rings that were a couple of orders of magnitude above my actual price range and fumbled one while putting it back. The manager picked it up, checking it briefly with his loupe, and steered me to the home furnishings when I said that she really wanted to spruce up the entry hall. From the corner of my eye I could see Clara come around a corner and give me a wink before turning to the clerk attending on her with a little shake of her head as if to say she couldn't believe they let dolts like me in.

The fun was just starting. Satisfied I was out of harm's way, the manager returned to the front counter. I gave it a minute and a half before wedging my foot between two heavy pieces of furniture, knocking over a pair of ornamental brass scales, dropping on my back and letting out a yelp as the metal hit the tile floor. There was plenty of noise to get everyone's attention, but I built on it, howling about my ankle. The manager came over, and as I began fussing about what my lawyer would have to say about this death trap of a junk shop, the clerks came, too, and Clara was guaranteed a bit of time to investigate unseen. They tried to dislodge me and I made it take longer by moaning in distress with their efforts and seeming to try to get myself out while undermining anything achieved. At last, I was on my good leg and being helped to hop over to a Victorian chaise lounge with a quasi-classical scene from Greek mythology embroidered on it. It was hideous. I pretended to like it, asking about the provenance and creator as they propped me up with some throw pillows.

To be honest, I was having a blast buffaloing

them while my partner played the snoop. The background checks I'd been doing for my client were mostly desk work and I'd been stuck in a uniform for years. This kind of undercover operation was a lot more fun. Clara came out of a back room and signaled me before leaving. I rolled up my trouser leg, remarked on the lack of swelling, gave it a few stretches and got up. The relief on the manager's face was palpable and he offered to send the awful chaise to my home, as a sign of his personal respect. That I had not expected. I hesitated a moment and then gave him the address of Eugene Marshall's apartment. It would be fun as a gag gift, and he might like the naked nymphs and satyrs, actually.

We repeated with variations at six other businesses. I was right about Louie Duvall. He insisted on examining my leg himself and remarked on how beautiful it was. I gave him an encouraging smile and asked how long he'd been in the art business. Clara had plenty of time to look around in that shop, even to check on me in the middle of things when Duvall was laughing a little too hard at one of my jokes. After she'd left there and I'd caught up with her, she actually asked if I'd given him my number. "No, but he wrote his home number on the back of this business card." I handed it to her. "Might be useful if the thieves turn up. Still nothing?"

"The only Russian items I've seen have been in the shops too long or had an impeccable provenance."

I nodded. "We'll try some more tomorrow. I have a friend in the fraud squad here who might know what places are most likely to have Russian items."

"I thought stores stayed open late in American cities."

"A few hours more," I said, "but I'm ready for dinner and I've fallen down enough times for the day. Plus, I have other clients. I need to drop off some work I've done for Eugene Marshall and get a list of new names from him."

"You know Eugene?" she asked, a little startled.

"*You* know him?" I asked back. I didn't exactly like that. He was a bit of a womanizer. She was in her thirties, like me, and I expected her to have experience. I just didn't like the idea of her possibly having had it with someone I knew.

"Professionally." Her tone made it absolutely clear that he had tried to turn it personal and failed. "He makes military supplies and equipment, Britain needed those things."

"Do you mind if we swing by there?"

"Of course not." She paused, "He's not bad, in his own way. I heard he didn't fire the women working for him after the war. He simply enlarged his workforce to hire veterans."

"Right. He's been going big on what they're calling the peace dividend. All these fellows coming home with savings from their service getting married— he opened a couple of factories to make materials for kit homes. He's got researchers working on better diapers because with all these marriages, that will be the next boom. He's also designing educational toys."

"An arms merchant focusing on baby care. I wonder how many paternity suits it took to get him thinking in that direction."

I was tempted to tell her the truth— that he's terrible with faces and has been paying, without a lawsuit or blood testing, for the raising of seven children. I'd suggested once that I could check on their whereabouts relative to his in the months preceding the birth dates, just to make sure it could be true, but he had said no. He'd rather support a woman and child who had lost or been abandoned by the father and driven her to a fib, than leave them on their own. He did insist on letters with photos of his (maybe) kids. But I figured the fewer people who knew about that peculiarity of his, the less likely he was to get misused.

"He likes kids," was all I said. I changed the subject back to our case. "Hey, about those thieves. You mentioned thinking they were involved in some murders? Tell me about it."

"There were two dock workers found in the water, dead, with severe lacerations on their necks. One was mentioned in a Vladivostok newspaper without much detail. The other was found in Vancouver, Canada six weeks later. Investigators determined he died before going into the water, apparently from an ice pick attack that pierced his artery. This was discovered two weeks before the first of the suspicious items, a Faberge egg, was entered in an auction house catalog."

"I can see why you're worried about what these guys will do to cover their tracks."

"That's not all. Four months later, there was a fire that took out a five-story apartment building in San Francisco, killing the owners and an uncertain number of occupants."

"You're relating that to this case?"

"The entire building had been rented to a Russian couple, who were apparently running an organization there. And the Russian district had some very high-value art pieces show up around that time without explanation."

"And so it might be arson to cover up more activity? Mass murder? This doesn't sound like it's just about unloading stolen art treasures."

"No, it doesn't," said Clara. "But it's why Interpol is involved, and can stay involved unless it becomes obviously political. The murders and the missing persons cases— upticks in those in the involved cities and some other potentially related sites as well— don't seem to be political. The dock workers weren't activists or anything. The landlady and her husband were a nice, semi-retired couple who were interested in their local community, good neighbor type volunteering, but nothing ideological. The missing persons cases aren't a new demographic. It's the usual: mostly vagabonds, prostitutes, and young people who might have just disappeared of their own accord. But for that reason, they're also the ones easily targeted."

"Still, I guess I'm taking over the investigation if we find out it is political and you have to drop it. Or you could quit your job and be a private eye, too."

"Not on my visa."

"You'd just dump it in my lap?"

"No, then I would get people in high places to put pressure on the proper authorities to take proper action."

"We're here," I said, pulling up near the Empire State Building.

"Does he always work late?"

"In a sense," I said. Officially, the building only rented out offices. But Eugene was Eugene and he had rented one floor for the office space, and another floor which had been converted half into a laboratory and half into a luxury apartment. I suspected he often forgot which half he was in if he didn't have either his domestic or scientific helpers nearby to remind him. "In his own way, he's hardly ever not working." As we walked to the elevator, Clara gave the place a good look. A surge of pride ran through me. She'd seen cathedrals and stately homes, maybe even palaces in Europe, but the glamorous Art Deco design and quality materials made this gem of American architecture the rival of any.

"What floor is he on?"

"The 43rd or 44th, depending on what he's doing."

"That's going to take rather a long time, isn't it?"

"Huh? No, these are high speed elevators." Well, I could be proud of the engineering at least, if the beauty didn't impress her. "Less than a minute. Wouldn't take much longer to get to the observation decks, if heights don't bother you."

"I can fly a plane, Mr. Jones. I've likely seen more spectacular views."

"They go by pretty quickly then," I remarked.

"Everything does," her voice was distant and sad for a moment.

I reached out and touched her arm, to offer what comfort I could and remind her of the here and now. I didn't know what she'd lost. I didn't need to. The world had been through close to two decades of unusually severe trouble. She patted my hand. And then we were on the 44th floor. There were still a few office workers on the job. Pearl Tanner, the afternoon receptionist, gave me a big smile. She had gray hair and blue cats-eye glasses frames that matched her eyes. "Rafael, you are a sight for sore eyes! Mr. Marshall is going to be so happy to see you. You're not going to believe this, but we had two resignations in this office just this week."

"You're kidding me," I said. She handed me a folder with the information on people they needed background checks on. "Did Sheila's boyfriend finally propose?"

"No such luck." Pearl leaned forward to confide, "These aren't even marriages *or* new job offers. Tammy and Irene both sent in letters of resignation because they found religion."

"That doesn't make any sense. Can't they work and go to church?"

"Oh, it's some kind of thing where they live there and study, like a way of life." She waved a hand in the air dismissively. "Catch me doing more than throwing a dollar into the collection plate on Christmas and Easter. I mean, religion may be good for the soul, but practicing it is tedious."

"Amen," I quipped.

"You can leave the reports with me, but go ahead and check in with Mr. Marshall. I think he has some other things to talk to you about and aren't you going to introduce me?" Pearl spoke fast and changed topics just as quickly. I set the reports on a corner of her desk while I introduced her and Clara to each other. "Miss Thomas is a new client, but she's already met Eugene."

Pearl tilted her head, "And you seem pleased to be here."

"I worked for the British government during the war. Martial Industries did some designs for us starting in 1939. I've never seen these offices;

we met in London and Washington."

"Sounds like we owe you for a growth spurt," Pearl smiled. "Back then, Martial Industries was mostly on paper and Marshall Enterprises had four factories."

"Next time I see Mr. Churchill, I will express your appreciation for the business."

I said goodbye to Pearl and showed Clara to the stairs, since it was just one floor while Pearl was still gobsmacked by the name-dropping.

"You really know Churchill?" I asked.

"My brother-in-law does. So I see him at parties sometimes." She shrugged.

It surprised me how nonchalant she was and I almost said something about not knowing anyone when I realized that I was taking her to see a multimillionaire via his back staircase. And there had been generals and VIPs during the war. Most people, no matter their resume, were just people once you knew them.

And with that in mind, we came to the private quarters of Eugene Marshall. If you ask me, there's too many guys who will tell you the Romans were great because they built structures that lasted for centuries, but who won't let an Italian-American architect join their country club. Eugene wouldn't think twice and would either forget entirely that the chap was Italian or ask him if he knew the secret of Roman concrete. Eugene spends at least 90 percent of his time meeting other people mind to mind. Just for a break, he sometimes met someone body to body, which was where the child support payments came in and also what the occasional basketball pickup game would fall under.

Of course, he wasn't going to meet anyone if I didn't remember my passcode to his apartment. Another invention of his, there was a numerical keyboard that would light up the name of the visitor corresponding to that code inside, after which we could be buzzed through. If we had come via elevator, we would have just knocked on a door, but this was quicker than the security ogre who would have answered. As it was, Eugene greeted us himself, throwing the entryway open. "Raf! So good to see you. And..." he looked at Clara a moment, "Miss Thomas?"

That surprised me. He was bad with faces. But hers was worth remembering. I haven't quite said yet what her mouth was like. Her lips were full, round, making her mouth into almost an oval when relaxed. They were smooth and moved expressively. A feature like that could stick in the mind of the most abstracted genius.

She gave him a nod. "Delighted to see you again," she said in a pleasant, but not truly delighted way. That was good for me: Eugene was tall, blond, and his blue eyes had a boyish innocence that could charm the ladies.

He looked over his shoulder. "Walter! Hide the ice buckets!"

I looked at her. "He needed cooling off the first time we met," she explained. "There was champagne chilling, so the bucket was handy."

"I may have said something about being aflame." Eugene acknowledged.

"And I'd come in search of arms for Britain, not hands," she concluded.

I shook my head at him. Sometimes his approach worked, probably because he was handsome, good-natured, and rich, and I make no assumptions on the weight of each factor. I think some of those girls are just right for him, too. You see, he's the opposite of me when it comes to relationships. I'm always hoping to meet that one girl who will see something in me that makes her want to be with me forever. I've fallen in love more times than I can count during that search, but whether it turns out she was just looking for a little fun or she was almost to the altar when she realized my late hours or inability to play the get-along-to-get-ahead games at work weren't going to change and weren't the future she dreamed of, I always ended up losing a little bit of my heart. Eugene, on the other hand, was completely lacking in romantic sensibility. It's not that he was using women, it's just that he assumed they, like him, are simply interested in the physical reaction and nothing more. When he was correct, that was good for both of them, I guess, but I always felt he was missing out by not feeling something more.

But, I wasn't here to talk about his personal life.

He led the way to where he kept a little bar and offered us a drink.

"Why not?" I said. "It's not like I have to worry about being on duty anymore. Bourbon on the rocks."

"Sherry, I suppose," said Clara.

Eugene poured for all and then told us, "I'd ask you to dinner, but I'm expecting my girlfriend to come around soon. To Katie's health!"

So much for not being there to talk about his personal life. "Girlfriend?"

"I know. I thought you'd fall in love again before I ever did, but there's just something about her..."

"Eugene, tell me everything. When did you

meet her?"

"About three weeks ago. I was at a Materials Conference when I bumped into this breathtaking beauty in the hotel bar."

"Oh, God," said Clara. I knew what she was thinking.

"Eugene, women who hang around places like that looking to meet men..."

"It's not like that," he said. "Honestly, I never thought you'd be the cynic. She's an art expert who was there in town to talk with a museum curator to give them some details on the history of some items in their collection. She's quite wealthy and cultured, and she has some very exciting ideas about how art intersects with engineering, and the importance of symmetry and proportions in both fields. I think we must have talked half the night away about crystal structures."

"What does an art expert know about crystal structures?"

"She's a refined lady. She likes her jewelry." I think I noticed Clara doing an eye roll, but I nodded.

"The structure determines how a gem will fracture, which determines what cuts are good for a stone, right?" I half-remembered that from geology in high school and a somewhat drunk colleague trying to explain something about a gemstone smuggling operation case he'd broken.

Eugene drew my attention back to the paperwork I'd been given upstairs. "I wanted to talk to you about those girls who resigned. Go ahead and do the background checks on our top candidates to replace them, but I want this new religion they joined investigated. One of them mentioned it's called the Order of Repentance. Find out what the leadership is doing. If it's some kind of scam, I owe it to my people to find out and warn them. If they want to come back to work here after, so much the better. Your usual rates, and a hundred-dollar bonus each if you can get Irene and Tammy back."

"Sounds good." We shook on it.

"I do hope this won't interfere with *our* investigation." Clara sounded a little frosty.

"Ooo! What are you working on?"

"It's basically a stolen property case..." As I started to explain, the doorbell rang. And by the ring of his doorbell, I mean a copy of King Kong's roar. "Sounds like Fay Wray has arrived."

Eugene's blue eyes got a faraway look I generally associated with his inventing process beginning. "Katie's here," he said warmly. He glanced into the mirror and gave himself a quick tidy-up.

"Oh, good, we'll get a look on our way out," Clara put her glass down.

I took the hint and led her to the front door. "It's really no problem," I mentioned. "I'm prioritizing your case; the thieves seem to be a lot more dangerous than some religious scam. I've dealt with things like that before."

We both put on smiles as we opened the front door. The woman standing in front of us had pale skin, red-gold hair, and a perfectly tailored green wool dress. I guessed she was about the same age as Eugene, that is to say around forty. That was nice; 'age-appropriate' was another concept he was weak on, and I knew he had probably dated about twenty years in either direction. She was tall, which was another way she'd go nicely with him. The lady ran her eyes over us briefly, then fixed her gaze on me.

"You must be Katie," I said. "We're friends of Eugene."

"A pleasure, I'm sure." She said it more as if she was sure it was a pleasure for us to call him a friend, rather than a pleasure to meet us. And yet she continued to stare at me.

"Well, I'm sure we'll be properly introduced later." I stepped aside and held the door open for her, then stepped out after Clara. Katie seemed a little strange, but maybe that was another reason she and Eugene were hitting it off. As we headed for the elevator, I offered. "We could go up to the observation deck now."

"I think not," Clara said.

"Why? Do you not want to hang out with me? You can't be bothered by heights if you're a pilot."

"No," she shook her head. "I think you're quite nice, actually, Rafael. It's... have you ever heard of the call of the void?"

"Is that one of those H.P. Lovecraft stories?" I asked.

"No. It's when a person is standing by a cliff or a window, and they get an impulse to jump. As if they believed they could fly, instead of encountering a short, sharp shock at the end."

"Oh."

"Yes. I don't get it in an aeroplane, because I *am* flying then. But I don't like to be standing on the edge of a building."

It was hard to imagine feeling that way, being that afraid of your own impulses, but I accepted it. "Well, let's go down to the streets, and I'll give you a walking tour. I know a place that does fish and chips takeaway," I said.

She smiled. "You remembered."

'I'd be a terrible investigator if I didn't remember the answers I get."

"Tell me something you are terrible at," she suggested.

I thought for a moment. "Knitting."

"Go on!"

"Really, I tried taking it up once. Thought it would be something to do when I was keeping surveillance on a place. I... got tangled up, just when I needed to take off driving and tail a courier."

"No!"

"I drove eleven miles snarled in a wool web, and it took me almost as long to unwrap myself so I could phone the location in as it did to drive there."

THE ELLIS ISLAND TRAFFIC CONTROL BOARD

The nice thing about walking with someone is it really gives you a chance to talk and it reduces stress so people discuss things a little more freely. Even so, Clara was more inclined to chat about the things around her than herself. I was a little surprised that the thing that struck her most about the city was how new all the buildings were, but of course, that was the difference between Europe and America. That, and how we were untouched by the war. "Did you travel much before the war?"

"I'm afraid not. The education of three girls was expensive, and I think there was some idea that one could meet bad influences going abroad."

"Bad influences, eh?"

"My parents wouldn't know a bad influence if he came with a good enough job and connections."

My brain switched gears very quickly. I'd seen

enough cases as a cop to recognize the tone of voice, the haunted look. "I hope the war wasn't kind to him."

"It wasn't. He was in the wrong place during an air raid. That actually made things worse for me for a while. Some people thought the right thing to do would be to go back and take care of him. It certainly delayed the divorce paperwork."

"Did you at least send a sympathy card?"

"To my estranged husband?"

"No, to whatever nurse ended up having to look after him. Guys like that don't change. Even if he can't hurt anyone physically, he'll go with verbal abuse, smears, and manipulation. In short, whatever makes him feel powerful."

"You sound like you know him."

"That kind doesn't vary much. I've come to think that there are more ways to be a good person than to be a bad one. Some day, if you feel like it, you can fill in the details. Until then—" Our discussion was interrupted as a small group of local residents came up to us. Clara was probably confused to find me suddenly subjected to hugs and kisses on my cheek— and that was from the men. Once the greetings, in half a dozen languages, subsided enough, I introduced her to them. "Clara, these are most of the founding members of the Ellis Island Traffic Control Board. They are some very dear friends of mine. They haven't seen me since before the war."

"Traffic control?"

"Sounds less serious than it is. These guys formed a civilian committee across many different immigrant communities to curb human trafficking. Since Missing Persons was my specialty, I was all for it and helped them. They helped me, too, more than I can say."

A plump, short woman whose dark hair had streaks of gray took hold of Clara's hands. "You are such a lucky girl, Clara!" she said.

I broke in quickly. "Tía Maria, ella no es mi novia. Estamos trabajando juntos para resolver un crimen. Es una mujer policía muy inteligente que necesita mi ayuda para encontrar a unos peligrosos ladrones y asesinos rusos."

"Bandidos de Rusia, de todas las cosas. ¡Los comunistas son terribles! Nunca deberíamos habernos aliado con ellos, pero nuevamente, ¿qué opción tuvimos con el Eje? Pregúntele a Ivan. Pregúntele a Ivan sobre estas personas terribles. Si alguien sabe qué es sucediendo en su comunidad, sería él, pero, por supuesto, no es así en absoluto, solía ser un periodista antes de la revolución."

Clara's brow furrowed with concentration. "Did you follow that?" I asked her.

"I'm not that good with Spanish She spoke so quickly."

"When I told her we're looking for Russian criminals, she reminded me that Ivan was a former newsman and still keeps his ear to the ground." Ivan Sokolov had, in fact, heard his name when Maria spoke it and stepped forward. He was probably the oldest one of the committee, in his late sixties, with a full, white beard. White hair also cascaded to his shoulders from under his hat.

"I do," he told us. "In Russian. In English... in English, my ears do not work so well."

"Right," I said. I explained to Clara. "He turned in his tips to me in writing. I think he had help to get it just right. We might need a translator."

She looked a little smug. "I'm almost as proficient in Russian as you seem to be in Spanish." She turned to Ivan and said something like, "Dobryy vecher. Spasibo, chto predlozhili nam svoyu pomoshch'."

"Hey," I pointed out. "If we're going to have a long discussion, let's go into that cafe over there and stay warm while we do it." It was April, so it wasn't awful out, but the night was drawing on and since we were on an island, every breeze brought a trace of moisture in the air. Clara translated that and they took my advice, though I had to stop for more hugs and handshakes from the team, who overall would rather go on with what they were doing that evening than listen in on an all-Russian conversation. Clara and Ivan ordered tea and madeleines. I ordered a cup of cocoa, because the events of the day had been stimulating enough. I didn't need caffeine.

While she was talking to Ivan, I went over to a beat-up old piano against the back wall. The thing about a hole-in-the-wall near Broadway was that they were used to musicians wanting to play just to share or keep in practice. So I knew the owner wouldn't mind if I played the blues quietly. Not that there was anything wrong with my mood, it was just a good time and place for something a little slow and introspective. It had been a while since I'd had the chance to tinkle around the keys and I guess I lost track of time as I varied up the bass line and layered on trills and snatches of melody from songs I loved. I was a little startled when Clara's warm voice asked, "Do you dance as well as you play?"

"There's only one way to tell," I said.

"Remember how I said I wouldn't go out with you to talk about joining Interpol? I'd only go out with you if I wanted to?"

"I definitely remember that. Tomorrow night, dinner and dancing somewhere nice?"

"I'd like that." We smiled together.

On the way back she told me what she'd learned. Ivan went around to places that carried vintage Russian items on a fairly regular basis because he met people who were sources of information. Sometimes, too, he could pick up some small reminders of his homeland. The important thing was that he'd spotted some jewelry at a storefront by Sheepshead Bay which he recognized as belonging to a princely family from a story he'd done about a wedding in the family back in his newspaper days. He'd hoped perhaps some surviving members of the family had made it to the U.S. and he had gone in to ask questions, but the manager had been very rude to him. He had tried just leaving a phone number so the sellers could get in touch with him, should they choose to, and still been rebuffed. While protecting clients' privacy can be important in many businesses, being rude to someone just wanting to leave a message was certainly suspicious. It wasn't politics, either— a shop that dealt in high-end goods would be friendly with the white Russians.

I dropped Clara off at her hotel with a plan to

meet in the morning and give The Silver Samovar a visit. She didn't wait for me to open her door, but popped out and came around to my side, then bent down to look at me. The window was down, so she reached in and touched the side of my face. "You're a very likeable guy, Mr. Jones."

"The feeling is mutual."

"I know. That's why I want you to stay in the car. I'm not quite ready for a first kiss."

So I let her walk herself into the hotel, admiring the walk and the woman, and musing on the implication in the phrase first kiss, that there would not only be such forthcoming, but it would be only the precursor to more unnumbered.

MOOSE'S MEMORY

I was all the more eager to see her the next morning and made sure my shave was impeccable and my curls tidy. I hadn't made much effort yesterday when I thought I was just going to be unpacking and arranging my office. The dull but proper business suit was a given, since we were going to another upscale shop. Clara came over bright and early so we could plan. It might have been wishful thinking on my part, but I thought she looked even prettier today.

Now that we knew we should be going to the right place and likely to find enough that the NYPD could get a search warrant to do it officially, Clara showed me how her purse also acted as a secret camera. The clasp area was richly ornamented with a metalwork design to hide the button that turned the clasp itself into an operating switch and the aperture. The idea was we'd go in as a couple, ask to see the jewelry, I'd start being a bit rude about the price on some piece, giving her a reason to "fidget" with her purse and take some good close photos of the jewelry. Combined with the newspaper photos showing them being worn by Russian nobles, we ought to be able to get the police to listen to Clara.

It was a fine spring day, We certainly weren't the only successful couple going down to the beaches of south Brooklyn to enjoy a stroll and a bit of shopping. This was definitely more enjoyable than most plainclothes work, and I began to wonder if I should give some thought to the job offer she'd brought up in the beginning. Not that I was sold on it, but it had some appeal. Working alone could be boring.

The Silver Samovar was bigger inside than it seemed outside, a narrow storefront, but running deep and going up to a second floor. They had a door on the right which probably led to space behind the hat shop next door. The tool sounds coming from behind it would be more befitting of a carpenter repairing an old piece of furniture than a milliner stitching on a bow.

Sauntering up to the counter with Clara on my arm, I asked the man behind the counter, to open the jewelry case and show us a few things. I mentioned I was looking for a few Easter presents and since my brother was marrying a Russian lady in June, I wanted to give Russian gifts as a sort of a theme. The man, a balding, shrewd-faced fellow by the name Adrian Petrov, said he was the manager and could help me find appropriate things. What price range was I looking for? I said I planned not to go above five figures... per item, and then only if it was really worth it.

The jewelry we were looking for was there, all right, among other sparklers and an enameled, gilded, and gem studded objet d'art that even my eyes knew was a Faberge egg. At that moment, I was happy the Russian aristocracy spent so much money on useless collectibles. Clara pointed at a pair of pearl and diamond earrings. "Your mother would love those!" she gushed.

"Maybe, maybe not." I nonchalantly began asking questions about where they came from and if they had been certified and graded by a professional jeweler. Clara had her purse out on the counter and her hands rested on it, relaxed. Then I asked about price. She rolled her eyes. The manager gave a figure. I said it was too much for an item without complete documentation. He insisted that a jeweler's authentication was all that was needed and we could arrange that easily if I doubted his word. I said jewelry has a story and did he bother to collect the stories for any of his stock. Clara fiddled with her purse as Petrov and I began to get fully into a debate. Our voices rose as we got heated, and if the purse camera clicked, I couldn't hear it.

We hadn't counted on how much disregard for the law the fence might have. Clara had just given me a little nod to tell me she was done taking photographs and I could wrap things up, when a hand that could have been used to argue that man was descended from grizzly bears fell on my shoulder. The arm that went with the hand continued the large and powerful motif, and the eyes I met suggested he'd just come out of hibernation to discover his cave was all out of coffee. But, dull though he might be, his memory worked just fine. Maurice "Moose" Boucher had come to America from Canada with a load of illegal hooch back in the day. He'd overstayed Prohibition and when I'd arrested him in 1934 he had shifted over to a nasty mix of robbery, theft, intimidation for hire, and pimping.

"This ain't no rich guy," he told the manager. "This is a cop."

"Ages ago," I said, "Before the war. I served in Europe and became an officer."

The manager quickly locked the jewelry cases back up. Without saying a word, he gave Moose a nod. Moose swung fast, but I ducked faster. He clipped the manager on the ear, but I doubt it did much. While I was low, I threw an elbow where it would do the most good. As he doubled over, I spun away and kicked him in the neck. Trust me, with a neck as thick as his, it wasn't going to do permanent damage, but it was enough to make him too dizzy to get off his knees right away. Too bad I had my eyes on him and not on the assistant who caught my ribs with a crowbar.

I staggered and realized I was going to fall over Moose if I didn't turn it into a roll, which I did, giving Moose another kick, catching him in the temple this time. He finished going down to the floor for a nap while I landed in a crouch on the other side of him. The guy with the crowbar swung it again, just in the air to get a better feel for using it as a weapon. He looked young enough not to have a lot of experience with this kind of thing and I wondered if I could close in. It would be risky; another hit with that thing could put me out of the fight myself.

I feinted a little to the right, the only sensible approach I'd have toward him, just to test his response. He was quick, but a nervous quickness.

I might be able to work with that, get him over-reacting until he left himself open. I grabbed a picture off the wall, and threw it at him, chest-level. He sidestepped, which was actually the best move, and I realized belatedly that would get him near where Clara had been standing.

My eyes must have widened, because he gave me a sneer to indicate he didn't think much of my current ploy. Except it wasn't a ploy, Clara, already well away from where I'd last seen her, had really just thrown a dagger which struck the guy in his left shoulder. He yelled and dropped the crowbar to try and paw the dagger out from the shoulder. She stepped up to him, put her hand on his throat and held concentrated pressure on it. "Leave the knife alone," she told him, "for your sake. It's lodged in the bone and you'll want a doctor to get it out without the pain being excruciating. Nod if you understand." He did. Apparently, her hold was impeding his ability to speak. "Do you know anything about the people who brought in the jewels? It doesn't have to be a name. Any kind of description would be a start." He shook his head. "Then we don't need you conscious." She held the grip forty seconds more and he fainted.

She looked at me. "The manager could have

been really helpful. But he was reaching for a gun."

I checked behind the counter. He was slumped to the floor with blood trickling from a gash on his temple. A clerk had had a plaster statuette broken on him and was making a whining sound. I surveyed the damage she'd done. "Code breaking, pilot, and this? Clara, were you in covert ops during the war?"

"What a ridiculous question."

"I think it's reasonable to wonder."

"But not reasonable to expect an answer. Think about it. Such a person would have been doing classified work with classified contacts. Some of their work would still be considered need to know only. They would have to be able to keep their mouth shut. So a person who had worked in covert ops would certainly say they had not."

"Did you work in covert ops?"

"I did not."

What a woman. It occurred to me that such a person would also possibly have more than one reason to be working a job with lots of international travel in her post-war career, but that would be a question too far.

She pointed out, "We should leave. No one's capable of talking right now, and we'll need to get the photos to the police quickly if we don't want all the evidence gone by the time they have a search warrant."

I reached over the counter, unlocked the case, grabbed the Faberge egg and a pair of earrings, and quickly hid them in places around the room. I gave her a wink. "You're absolutely right."

Once we were out of there, she held my hand and I held my side as we walked briskly to where my car was parked. "I need to get the photographs developed," she stated. "How badly were you hit?"

"I'll be sore on that side a couple of days. Nothing to worry about."

"Are you sure?"

"I always recover fast. My mother says our family has a gift for healing."

"Not everything heals on its own."

"Well, I guess I'll find out what doesn't one day, but right now, I'm still planning on dancing with you tonight."

"Then at least have a nap or something while I throw together a makeshift darkroom."

"Can I be in the dark room with you?"

"You'd only get in the way. But if you don't mind me setting up in your bathroom, you can be nearby."

Not exactly the flirtation I was going for, but

companionability would be nice. And the crowbar had done enough damage that sitting quietly with a cold compress on it, maybe some ice, wouldn't be a bad idea to get me through the rest of the day. She needed some basins and other things that I didn't have but there was a five and dime down the street and she had the chemicals and papers she needed in a case she'd brought along.

I turned on the radio, found a station with some big band music, turning the volume down from my usual setting so we could talk over it easily. After running some cool water on a washcloth, I turned the bathroom over for her to make into a darkroom. Since she had to keep the door closed to keep out the light, I went ahead and stripped down to my waist to examine the injury. The bruising was deepest right over a rib, but my jacket kept the skin from being torn and while a fracture was possible, there couldn't be a complete break. I added some ice to the cloth and stretched out on the living room floor because I didn't have that many furnishings yet.

While I didn't mean to fall asleep, with the sound of "Moonlight and Roses" and quiet noises from the adjoining room, I found myself relaxing and it seemed like seconds later that I woke to Betty Hutton singing "Doctor, Lawyer, Indian

Chief" and Clara washing out the basins with the bathroom door open. I had just enough time to get dressed again and back on my feet before she came out.

"Feeling better?"

"Yes, I am." I took a deep breath. The ache had faded quite a bit. "How are the photos?"

"The similarity between the items and the newspaper photos is evident in one of the pictures and a couple of others really capture the quality. I got a good one of the Faberge egg, too. I made two sets of prints, so we can hang on to our own set while getting these to the police."

"And the negatives?"

"Secret compartment on my person."

"Is there anything you don't do well?" I asked, opening the door for her.

"Yes, actually. I can't play the piano past 'Chopsticks'. My childhood form of rebellion was to ditch every music lesson I could manage."

CLARA PROVED ME WRONG

The police station was busy, crowded, and yet boring. There were winos trying to have extended conversations with their booking officers because it was the first time in a couple of days someone was making eye contact with them. The hotel-room thief maid, the lunchtime barroom brawlers, and the shoplifters were all a dime a dozen, processed almost mechanically by the guys at their desks. I went to the duty officer's desk and asked for Roger Sloane, the detective Clara had spoken to on the phone. Of course, she'd take the lead once we got to him, but since I knew local procedures, it made sense for me to get us in.

The duty officer made a call, then had us wait in a seating area until he got a return call when Sloane was ready for us. He gave me an office number. We headed down a corridor and up a couple of flights of stairs to where the more administrative work took place. Sloane was part detective, part bureaucrat. I knew him more by reputation than through interactions from my days in the force. He got on with people more powerful than he was, and didn't make waves but could efficiently run a team on a complex investigation. He'd been dealing with things like organized crime, forgery rings, and money laundering for years. He didn't waste resources on operations that weren't going anywhere, which made him efficient and yet was probably the reason why he hadn't been enthusiastic about trying to make a case for art smuggling and thievery out of a few pieces sold in this city and some tenuously connected crimes thousands of miles away.

All of which is to say, I went in with a professionally cordial attitude and expected to hang back while they started on a plan. She introduced herself to him in person for the first time and I showed him my license and explained I was here as a private detective helping Interpol collect information, and that I could be excluded at any time.

"You're darn right you can. But you can stay with your client for now." So far so good, right? His tone of voice was a little aggressive, but what cop hasn't had a bad day and ended up sounding off? I stepped back and listened while she told him about The Silver Samovar and the princely jewels that had turned up a short time before.

To my surprise, he told her there was still nothing worth investigating. "Those Russian nobles, they smuggled out what they could. If they couldn't get themselves out, half the time they gave paintings and furs and jewels to their servants, just to spite the Reds. I don't blame them. The commies stole everything they had. I'm sorry I didn't make my stance on this to you clear enough before, sweetheart. As I see it, what good is investigating going to do? Worst case scenario, there is no crime as any American would see it, and we hassle some nice immigrants or visitors for no reason. Best case, you prove there was a crime, we collect the treasures, and then what? You swan back to Russia with them and give Stalin a couple of millions worth of treasure to spend on bombs and tanks?"

I stepped forward then. "We don't decide whether the people who get their stolen goods back deserved them or not in the first place. If we don't do that with our fellow citizens, what makes you think you have the right to do that to a country? This isn't about helping Stalin. It's just doing our— your job as a law enforcement officer. There are international laws that we— you— have to respect whether you like it or not!"

"That's just what I wanted today, to get told my job by an ex-cop who dropped his job because he could never be a team player."

I hadn't expected that reaction. Neither had Clara. I let his words hang in silence a minute, then reminded him. "I wanted to join the army. Because I was 'essential personnel', they didn't want me. I had to quit to enlist. There was a war on."

"Oh, yeah, really brave. We of the NYPD were fighting Eye-ties at home in the form of Mafia, and they have better guns than we do. You were rounding up drunks and cowards."

That hurt. It wasn't what I had enlisted for, but it was the job I was assigned on account of my experience in law enforcement. It was more complicated than he made it sound, but I hadn't liked it. There wasn't much to say, I thought, but then Clara proved me wrong.

"If that's how you feel, if you'd been in his boots, I doubt you'd have written letter after letter asking to be reassigned to combat duty. Nor would you likely have had the initiative to break the case that got him into CID," that was the Criminal Investigations Division, "and you would *never* have taken a bunch of tired guards, shaken translators, lawyers, and clerks from at least half a dozen countries and turned them into a law enforcement organization on the fly with strong morale and the ability to calm traumatized victims and nervous turncoats, leading to rock-solid cases against the worst criminals in history!"

I think that was the moment it really dawned on me that she saw me as some kind of hero, in spite of my lack of action in the field. I might have blushed a little. I know her face was flushed.

Then he said to me, "You seriously asked for combat duty, Killer?"

"There was a war on!"

He laughed. Then he reached into his desk drawer, took out a folder, pulled a photo out of it and threw it on the desk. He'd kept us waiting just so he could get my old personnel file, I surmised. Clara looked at it, then looked inquisitively at the two of us glaring at each other. It was a shooting range target, shots neatly grouped around the shoulders and hip joints. A demonstration of a constant difference of opinion I had with standard training, which I had been disciplined for more than once.

I explained quietly, "The Killer thing is a joke because I say that a dead suspect can't answer questions."

"No, it's because we wanted you to understand you could get a partner killed trying to play nice with a hood."

"I never got a partner killed."

"No one wanted to work with you." That had been true in Buffalo, at one point, but I had friends still in the NYPD.

"And I think we'll have to manage to work without you. Good day, Mr. Sloane." Clara's tone was anything but gracious with that, but it made it easy to leave without punching a cop, which has never been a good idea, no matter how much he's asking for it. She led us out of the building in a fast march, but she gave me no doubt of who she was blaming for the awkwardness as she muttered about some people not knowing a sense of ethics if it fell on their incredibly thick heads.

"Are we going to manage to work without him?" I asked, once we'd gotten out of there.

"Maybe I can get state or federal officials to take an interest. I imagine jurisdictional issues can be worked out. Or someone else in his department who would like a promotion. I doubt he's a very popular man with his peers."

"Right. Tomorrow, you want to try your connections while I try mine?"

We agreed on that, and we went back to my place because she'd brought her evening wear along in case we ran late. She changed in the bathroom and I fixed myself up in my bedroom. I also did a quick tidy around the room just in case.

NOT JUST A SPARK

We went to a nightclub called The Peacock Strut, a nice little Manhattan spot that mixed their menus, cocktails, play-lists and clientele with enthusiasm. That's the best sort of place in my book, because jazz doesn't color inside the lines. I was looking swell in a suit of forest green with a bronze silk tie. She was radiant in a cocktail length royal blue silk gown. It didn't matter what else had happened that day, everything was perfect because of this moment. Although, come to think of it, knowing I'd found someone equally ready to defend with me in a physical or social confrontation made it even better.

For dinner I went with roast chicken, something not too heavy, since I intended to make proper use of the dance floor. While we ate, we talked about our pasts. It seemed like Sloane's attempt to shame me in front of her had the side effect of really breaking the ice. I talked about the first time I got into trouble with my fellow officers of the law over taking 'protect and serve' too seriously, refusing to modify a report to cover up for someone panicking at the sound of a backfire down the street and shooting a 15 year old kid who had a knife in his hands. We'd been called on a domestic because a neighbor complained about the sound of yelling and breaking dishes in the kitchen next door. Three cars were in the area and we called for the people inside to come out. The kid stepped out, knife in his hand. He'd been peeling potatoes, as it turned out afterwards. He and his grandma had been yelling at each other over his grades, while she was doing the washing up and he'd sassed her and gotten a few things thrown at him before being set to peel spuds. A kid, killed because someone spooked. Yeah, no one wanted to work with me after that, and someone noticed that the kid's family, besides me and my mom, were practically the only Latinos in Buffalo, NY, so that was the cause of some speculation that my biases were behind my refusal to play along on the report and say he shot at us.

I got put on the missing persons desk almost as a kind of punishment, so no one would have to be my partner and because no one at the department seemed to think it was an important job. It was the

Depression. People left in search of a job. In search of a new home. Or they just left because they couldn't take not providing or being provided for. Or they'd gone into a river in winter and not floated back to the surface while anyone was watching. The guy before me mostly just filed the reports. I didn't. I researched and researched and eventually, I got a lead on most of them. But I also took into account some people had a reason not to be found. Quite a few women I found but reported that I didn't, so I guess I wasn't totally adamant about honesty, just the serve and protect feature of the job.

Which led to Clara telling me more about her past. The whirlwind romance after meeting her husband-to-be at a golf resort. I asked if she played and she said she was there to learn but hadn't liked it much. She'd been bored. Charles Arden had been interesting. Fascinating, in fact. She hadn't realized at the time he was so good at telling stories about himself because he was so practiced in it. "I was young, naive. I took him at face value, and he was very good at having a high face value because it was really all he ever cared about. He needed people to admire him. I was drawn in. He showered me with attention at first, and made all the silly gestures like sending roses.

It was flattering and I thought he was showing me love. But he's not capable of it. He just wanted me to love him."

I put my hand on hers. I wasn't sure what to say, but she gave a little laugh. "Everyone wants to be loved. That's not a problem. It's the person who gets nasty when it isn't a constant stream, who needs to control not only the actions but the thoughts of people around them so they never feel criticized or need to compromise to make the other person happy... that's the problem type."

I laughed then. "If you want to lead on the dance floor, I'll follow."

"Let's not be quite that avant garde."

With Clara in my arms, I hardly felt the ache in my side from where the crowbar had hit me. I hadn't been sure how many dance styles we'd have in common, but Britain had picked up America's dance fashions with enthusiasm. She even knew some of the Latin styles, and wasn't too demure to give her hips the proper roll when we danced the rhumba as they played *Begin the Beguine.*

She could hold her own on the fast dances, unsurprisingly, and those were usually my favorites. I guess I'm a bit of a show-off, since a quickstep or Lindy hop can cut down on the number of couples on the floor and give the best dancers a chance to shine. When you've got a beautiful gal with you and she knows how to move with you, it's only natural to want everyone to see. With Clara, though, I was happier on the slow numbers, so I could keep most of my focus on her and only give a little attention to the floorcraft. Her story had more surprises to unfold. Thomas was (obviously) not her husband's name, but it wasn't her family name, either. Her brother-in-law had set it up as a cover identity for her and she liked it so much she'd had her name legally changed.

As much fun as we were having, especially on the tango, which had been so passionate we simply spontaneously kissed at the end of it, there were things to do and people to contact tomorrow, so we didn't stay until closing. That was probably just as well, because the crowbar injury was gradually wearing down my energy, but I covered that up pretty well.

I offered to drop her off at her hotel again, but Clara said she'd rather stop back at my office. "I left a few things there. I can call a cab after." That was fine with me. The hotel wouldn't be much of a place to end the night. Hotel detectives (a job for those who can't keep their small minds focused on their own business) don't like when guests who registered a room for one bring someone of the opposite sex upstairs with them. I wouldn't have said no to a goodnight kiss in the lobby, but it would be awkward to have an audience.

She'd stashed her bag in the office before we left, and after I unlocked the door, she hung up her coat, so it seemed like she'd just wanted a reason to come back. I hung mine up, too, and asked if I could pour her a drink. Before I finished the question, her arms were around my neck. I responded with enthusiasm and we got into a hot make-out session. We got swept up in the moment and before long, our shirts were unbuttoned, the better to touch and kiss and feel skin on skin. Then knickers hit the floor, our hands ended up messy, and we nuzzled and laughed and murmured sweet things through the clean up. Clothes rearranged, I suggested she forget the hotel, come upstairs, take a good hot shower and spend the night.

"I'd love to, really," she said, "but this case isn't the only assignment I have to manage. I've been away all day and I really do have to check my messages and find out what else may need my attention."

"Okay, I'll take you back..."

"We'll end up forever lingering in the car. I don't want to go and you don't want me to, but it simply must be done, so I'm going to call a taxi now before we can make it any harder for ourselves." She picked up the phone, and I played with the back of her neck while she gave the taxi company the address. When she was done, she told me, "We've got five more minutes for snogging, and if you want to have breakfast with me, you can meet me at the hotel restaurant at 9:00 AM."

It wasn't a bad way to end a night, and I wish it had ended just like that. Instead, I'd gone upstairs, taken a lonely shower, and was drying off when the phone rang.

"Hello?"

"Raf, it's me. I *did* have messages waiting. I have to go to Washington tomorrow on a early morning flight. I'm sorry. I'm sure I can get things wrapped up there in a few days, but we're trying to establish working relationships on several fronts, and —"

"—and you're a young agency and everyone's probably trying to do three jobs right now."

"I've got experience."

"It's crucial with NYPD giving you the brush-off right now." I sighed. "It's going to be like this for a while. Look, we can manage. I'll try getting you some unofficial help with the local force..."

"...I'll do the work in Washington and see if the

FBI can take an interest. And politics is forbidden to Interpol, but if I talk to certain people who work in intelligence and they are motivated by the possibility the perpetrators are moving information as well as artifacts, I can't help what they think."

"That's the spirit." I paused. "We can make this work. Call me. I'll try and get that job for Eugene wrapped up while you're away, too."

"Maybe..." she said, "maybe if things go well in Washington. Well, Interpol is under the umbrella of the UN. It might make sense to have a branch office in New York."

"That would be nice. And I'd want to see how I like working on my own for a while but, well, in a few months, if Interpol is still interested..."

"I'm sure the option will be given." She sounded happier by now, and I was feeling better, too, but still, I wanted more time together, a chance to really feel like a couple and not just a spark. I didn't know yet how trivial the distance between us would be compared to what was going to happen.

CULT FOLLOWING

The next day was deeply overcast, matching my mood. I started the morning by sending out some inquiries to start the background checks on Eugene's potential hires. After that I headed out, picking up bagels and cream cheese and going into the break room back at my old precinct.

I wasn't without friends there, even after the turnover and the issues Sloane had brought up. Flannery was still working there, and he was older than me and restless about getting to a higher rank. He scored very poorly on written exams, which didn't make much sense since he knew the laws and procedures quite well and actually followed them closely. He told me once that it took him a long time to read the questions and he always ran out of time. He held out hope that a really big bust might get him a little more leeway on the test scores.

I told him the whole story. As I thought, he was

more than a little interested in the case. Besides checking out The Silver Samovar (with the locations I'd hidden the suspect items noted down) with a buddy and investigating there, he was going to find out if there were any deaths or suspicious absences of dock workers. The nearly identical deaths in Russia and Canada bothered him.

"You want to go back to the Samovar?" he asked. "If we can't get anything else, assault charges could give us a reason to hold Moose and offer him a chance to talk."

"I'll identify him in a line up and press charges, but I've got another case going on and you don't need me in the shop for that bit— he'd just slip out the back if he saw me coming."

"Right you are. In fact, he's probably already skipped, since he's had a day. Maybe not, though, we can try. What's this other case of yours?"

"Not of police interest right now. Some cult, the Order of Repentance, has gotten a couple of people I know and a mutual friend is paying me to try to get them out."

"How?"

"The only way: try to get them to leave willingly. If I can find evidence of malfeasance that they can't explain away, these ladies aren't going to stay. Have you heard anything about people filing any complaints on them yet?" He shook his head and I continued. "These ladies are smart, respectable women. In fact, I'm surprised they got sucked in in the first place." I shrugged, "Maybe they were lonely."

"Or feeling a little lost after the war. Hits men more, but it's getting women, too. Three years ago, my sister was a factory foreman, now she's slinging hash because the war cost her her husband and the peace cost her her job."

"That's rough." I gave him Eugene's business card. "This is my client on this case. Have her send her resume there if she doesn't mind relocating. He's got multiple factories and he might have something in her line."

He pocketed it. "Can't hurt to try. And if you find anything illegal on that cult, Jones, anything at all, you give me a call. The laws give those scam artists leeway, but if they cross the line, we'll be happy to shut it down."

With that in mind, I found out what was going on with Irene through the subtle stratagem of asking the phone operator to get me through to a new church called the Order of Repentance, waiting until someone picked up, and asking to talk to Irene Milner. She agreed to meet with me in half an hour and gave me the street address. I asked her if she thought Tammy would like to meet me, too. She told me Tammy had left for a spiritual retreat in the Adirondacks. I was disappointed, but it might be easier to just work on one of them and if I could get her out of the cult, she might be able to influence the other.

We met at a diner. I saw Irene coming in in a plain black dress that didn't exactly flatter a warm blonde with gray eyes. Irene had been made for pastels, but I guess that wasn't spiritual enough. The waitress was clearing a booth for us just then, so I went ahead and ordered coffee for two. It looked like she could use a pick-me-up. "How are you doing?" I asked with genuine concern as she joined me. She was a little pale, and rather subdued.

"I'm well," she said, in spite of the evidence against it, "and very happy. I feel like I finally understand what God wants for me, and what bliss it can bring."

"Faith is a strong healer," I said amiably. "Of course, I thought you looked happy before, back at the office. Only twenty-eight years old and head of purchasing for the civil division."

"That was material success. I have found that what lies in the heart is more important."

"I can understand where you're coming from on that. But it's important that everyone's heart be in the right place, isn't it?" The waitress came then and we ordered. Irene was just going to have a cup of tea at first, but I pressed her to eat. She really did look pale. Was she ill? That could be a reason to take up religion so hard. "That's why I want to know about the leaders of this organization. If their hearts are in the right place, Eugene and I can rest assured you're in good hands. We do want you to be happy. But I don't want you to be mistreated. If you could help me get in, see what is happening at the Order of Repentance, I can report back to him that everything is fine, if it is. If it isn't, if anyone is being held against their will or if the place is a cover for any kind of criminal activity, well, you'd want to know, wouldn't you? Not that it's likely but..."

"I know what you mean. It's easy, isn't it, for a con artist to throw a coat of religion on a scam. I wouldn't stay for that. No, what you're asking for is fair, Rafael. You're named for an angel, you know? The angel of healing. Our holy man is a healer, too, and he's the real deal. You'll see. I'll give you a chance to take a good look around, but I think you'll find that what we have is so special, you'll want to join us."

"That's a possibility," my mouth said cheerfully. My brain, on the other hand, thought 'In a pig's eye' would be more accurate. "Is there anything special I should do to blend in?"

"I can offer you some extra acolyte's robes when you get there. You'll need to come around after work hours as my visitor. Honest labor strengthens the spirit as well as the body. Both are needed to serve God's plan."

I tried not to let the urge to roll my eyes show on my face. Irene had been kind of a happy-go-lucky gal. Smart as a whip, of course, but quick with a smile and a joke. This dull solemness was an entire different person, and it seemed her spark of life had been diminished. "Right, which would be what hours exactly?"

"Yes, of course. Well, our services are held as a midnight mass, so we don't begin work hours until 9 AM."

"9 to 5?"

"Very traditional." A hint of a smile played at her face for a moment, as if she at least remembered what it was like to laugh, hidden in the mists of time one week ago.

"I'll be there." We finished the meal companionably. Her mind often seemed to wander miles away, but I kept up light chatter about the news of the world and of the office and every once in a while with both she'd perk up and say something pertinent and not about religion. It gave me hope.

Having parted with her and no welcome until after five, I thought I might as well fill in Eugene about my cult investigation plan and let him know to cross off two of his potentials. One was a dishonorable discharge, and the other had lied about their college. That left ten I was still following up on.

When I reached his office, they told me he'd been in his lab since before eight in the morning. I got down there and the regulars there were all proceeding with routine tests, like whether a fabric made to be water repellent would also repel oils or compounds high in sugars or proteins. "Are you pouring blood on that swatch?" I asked a scientist, I think her name was Diane. She nodded. Seemed gross, but I had lost a few jackets to bloodstains that wouldn't come out. You should have seen the other guy's wardrobe, though.

I went on into Eugene's private lab. Unsurprisingly, he was standing by a table, writing on a notebook. He looked like he'd been up all night. Katie sat on a stool next to him, wearing a light green dress and an expression of mild boredom. Unlike Eugene, who was lost in whatever project he was working on, she noticed me and brushed Eugene's arm with her hand. Once he turned to her, she nodded in my direction. Following her gaze, he saw me and smiled. "Raf! What brings you here this evening?"

"It's afternoon, Eugene. Early afternoon."

"It is?"

"You got some idea for a way to suppress fire," Katie said. "You've been working on it for hours. I've been so proud of you. You have such a passion for your work."

"Way to go," I added, as much for Eugene finally having a romantic connection as for his efforts at invention. Somehow it made me feel less worried about whether Clara and I could keep love alive in spite of work conflicts. "I know that you've been moving away from military contracting since the war ended, but fire suppression improvements would be really useful for the services. You might see if you can get a research grant."

Katie looked a little surprised. "Are you a military man?"

"I was. Discharged a few months ago. Not a hero. More sort of a glorified guard."

"A guardsman? How old are you?"

"Really military police. I'm 35." I felt a little annoyed. "I wasn't put in the job because I was older than the other men, but because I came in with police experience."

"I told you about him, Katie," said Eugene. "We met when he found where a missing shipment of arms was headed and I was needed for the official recovery proceedings. He's a good man."

"I believe he is. Reliable?"

"I'd trust him with my life."

"All the same don't go risking it," she said, cupping his face in her hand and kissing his cheek. "I have so many plans for our future. But it is getting late. I should be going. You get some sleep, too." As he murmured his goodbye, she gave me one last look. "Goodbye, guardsman. Perhaps we will meet again." She picked up an umbrella leaning by the door and left with just the right amount of sway in her step.

She was definitely odd, but seeing her with Eugene, it was a little easier to understand them as a couple. With her gone, he was less distracted and I brought him up to speed, not just with the work I was doing for him, but telling him about Clara and me.

"Sounds like you're in love again."

"Yeah. I know, I said I'd make it to the end of

June without doing that." I took a fiver out of my wallet and gave it to him. "You know me too well. The question is, is she in love with me?"

"Sounds like it, if she's trying to transfer here. I suppose she could just be in love with the city, though."

"Thanks."

"New York does that to people."

"I hadn't even considered it. Look, if she means it about trying to get stationed here, then I'm sure she likes me, but what if she's just saying that to let me down easy? I thought everything was going so great, but suddenly she has to go off to D.C.?"

"You were getting new assignments all the time while you were in the army."

"Yeah, but—"

"How much notice did you get?"

"Depended on the circumstances." Eugene was being more rational than me. He often was. We were good for each other that way, I was more normal, but he was, in his own way, often more realistic. "You're right. There's nothing implausible about it. I'm just being silly because I've been dumped before when I thought things were going well. But this time, it's the real deal. We understand each other."

"If you do, why are you asking me about her?"

Eugene shook his head. "Want to see my fire suppressant? It's a system that runs pipes along the wall low, just about ground level, and if activated, it will release foam throughout every floor of a structure, be it building, ship, or it could even be built into an engine. The foam will fill up to about waist level and if the fire is higher, anyone nearby can easily throw the foam onto the flames. I'm just trying to determine the perfect chemical compound to use for it. It has to be mild enough for skin contact, do minimal damage to the structure it's protecting, and stop all kinds of fires."

I got dragged into that willingly enough, even though my knowledge was pretty much limited to using baking soda or a large lid to put out a kitchen fire instead of throwing water on it. He said the foam was pretty much the same thing; in each case, the idea was to deprive the fire of oxygen. The trick was to not deprive people of oxygen at the same time, or you'd save the property but risk higher loss of life. His foam would also be nonconducting and end up acting as a temporary insulator if the problem came from a short circuit. "Funny thing, Katie didn't seem to understand why I was so concerned with leaving enough space for people to breathe."

"Eugene, can you give me some information on her? An address?" It wouldn't hurt to run a background check and make sure he wasn't dating Lizzie Borden or something.

"I'm not sure. She doesn't live locally. She's staying at a hotel."

"Which one?"

"I'm not sure. She always comes here."

"What's the phone number?"

"I don't have it."

"How do you invite her over?"

"She calls. Or she just shows up."

I silently took a piece of scotch tape and lifted a print, likely thumbprint, from the wineglass she'd left behind in his lab. I might not be a cop anymore, but I couldn't help thinking like one, and a mystery woman dating a millionaire military contractor merited an investigation, even if I didn't have a client for it.

We talked a little more, but Eugene was looking tired, so I bid him farewell and went back to my office. I called in to my message service and found out Lieutenant Thomas had called and left her phone number. I gave it a dial. She was out, of course. I left a message at the front desk. Said Flannery was following the lead. Gave his contact information as well as mine. I wished I was talking to her and not a hotel clerk, because there were so many things I wanted to say to her that wouldn't be right for a message. In the end, I just said I'd be out that evening but she should be able to reach me the next day.

After that, I did some unpacking, went out to a lonely but early dinner at a diner where the waitress looked a bit like my first fiancee, the one who left because she'd never really been an adult on her own and needed to learn who she was before she could be sure she loved someone else, and relationships weren't built on heroics, which took me on a trip down memory lane that I really didn't need when I was worried about where Clara and I were going. There should have been a slow saxophone solo or blues piano on the radio instead of singing cowboys and sentimental crooners. Heading out to meet Irene at the cult's monastery was almost a relief. I had a knack, at least, for finding what was hidden.

The Order of Repentance had leased out, or had been donated, an old hotel. It was six stories high, on a corner to a narrow little street that probably hadn't even been named. The last time the exterior had been painted, it had been painted white, but that had been a long time ago, probably just before the Depression. The paint that remained was grimy and where it peeled away, cinder block was revealed. I guess the surroundings would help people put away worldly ideas, but price was probably the main reason to take it

The main entry had double doors, and a lobby with simple folding chairs and tables where initiates could meet with outsiders. The front desk was still operating as a reception area where a couple of members acted as staffers, writing names down, signing for packages. They were pleasant but remote, not making eye contact or connecting with visitors, only recording and announcing them. There were also eight men that I counted who didn't look at all friendly, standing by the inner or outer doors or walking between the tables.

Irene met with me and passed along a brown paper parcel. One of the guards glanced at us as he strolled by, but made no objection or inquiry. I patted her hands and reminded her that I wasn't here to cause trouble, but to put all worries to rest. She looked tense, regretful, and I didn't want fear hanging over her the whole time I was there.

The public section had a bathroom and I went in and put on the robes Irene had borrowed for me. I put them over my clothes, noticed in the tiny mirror that the low cut made my jacket and shirt visible underneath, and unbuttoned and tucked until I looked like the acolytes in the lobby.

Having talked my way into the sanctuary, I found it unsettling. I walked past several people "meditating" as they worked. I've heard that the idea of meditation is to empty the mind of thought, and they seemed to have done that quite well. Their expressions were slack. I'd seen that look sometimes before. A few combat fatigue cases where the person had just 'gone away', a neglected baby that hadn't learned to look to people for interaction, a boxer who'd been clocked and was on his way to the floor of the ring— they could look that empty. It wasn't healthy. I wondered if there were drugs being used on them. Maybe opium could do that, but it would take enough to be dangerous. Most drug users I saw were in their own heads, but they were still there.

Speaking of unhealthy, they were all pale, except for a few who were not capable of being pale, but were ashy. The ones working in the courtyard, taking little herb plants out of nursery pots and planting them in compact plots of freshly turned soil looked like they might have a few days worth of dirt on them and their robes. I saw a couple of elderly people as I made my way along, trying to keep my own expression neutral, but most of the acolytes were young, and the majority were female. I wanted to find some kind of office or private rooms for the leadership, because that would be where I might find paperwork that would show what was really up. I had a feeling there were newly made wills for the elderly, maybe signed already, maybe not. I expected to see some of the acolytes doing work that would obviously be salable for the prophet's profit, but they were stitching more of the robes for the order, painting the walls a sterile white, or the aforementioned gardening. I walked briefly through a kitchen, too. There was a woman making a large pot of soup and nothing else. It hardly looked enough to feed the people I'd seen already, and I hadn't even seen the leadership. Maybe they ate out. I noticed a cask of wine on one of the plain wooden tables, and dripped a bit on my finger for a taste. It wasn't good. Whoever bought it had no palate whatsoever or didn't drink it themselves and so didn't care. The soup had looked unappealing, too. The cook had been cutting up liver to put in it.

It might be a religious thing, again, mortifying the flesh with food and drink so dismal there would be no temptation to overindulge. The sparse, utilitarian furnishings I'd seen led some credence to that. I thought about it. The place seemed too spartan. Shouldn't there be some iconography, at least? Something decorative in the garden, if only something from nature to aid contemplation? The robes seemed weird, too. They were cut to the waist, showing some suggestive cleavage on the women, and everyone wore a sort of choker-like neck band with something I supposed was the cross, but it had three bars rather than one across, and the lowest was crooked.

I found a sort of gathering room next. There were no seats, just a ring of pillows with blankets spread across the circle. I was uncomfortably certain this was some kind of sex cult. I could see some white stains on the bedding, and rusty brown, too. I wondered how Irene could have gotten mixed up in a place like this and, for that matter, why she'd been willing to let me investigate if it was obviously this weird.

"Good afternoon," a warm and oddly familiar voice said.

I looked up. Standing in the double doors of the main entrance to the room was Eugene's strawberry-blonde girlfriend. "Katie?" I said in disbelief. She wasn't wearing the robes of the acolytes, I noted with some relief, but rather a black satin gown.

"Mr. Jones, you have as much curiosity as any cat. I hope you don't experience the same problems as the feline."

"What?" I was trying to sort out why she was here. That and the two women recruited from Marshall's office was making this look like a plot against him.

"Never mind. Come to me," she said. It sounded less like an invitation than a command.

She didn't seem to have a pistol or anything so I said, "No thanks. I try not to get too close to my friends' girlfriends when I'm around an orgy pit. It saves on misunderstandings."

"I said to come here!"

I took a step away from her at that. She sounded like she was angry that I didn't do what she wanted the first time, and her eyes had a strange gleam. Another drug, I wondered? Not inducing a stupor like the other people were showing, but maybe a kind of mania. "And I said no thanks. I'll give your regards to Eugene." I turned to go back the way I'd came, thinking it was a shame I couldn't investigate more undercover, but knowing the thing to do was warn Eugene and Martial Industries that there was some kind of security threat based in this Order of Repentance cult. Unfortunately, I found the way back was blocked by a number of the people who I had walked by without them appearing to pay me any attention before. They still had slack expressions. I said with a kind of forced cheerfulness, "You know, I wasn't properly invited here. I mean, I was sort of, but not by the owner, so you could call the police and have me arrested for trespassing." The group wasn't armed, except that a couple of them still had their shovels for gardening, and there shouldn't have been anything intimidating about drugged young women in V-neck robes, but I had a feeling in the pit of my stomach that I was in danger.

I turned back to Katie. She was now looking me eyeball to eyeball. I hadn't even heard her footsteps. "Obey me," she said.

"I've been discharged from active duty," I said, "and I don't even believe you're an officer. So why should I obey you?"

"I am a noblewoman," she was trying to sound seductive again. It was a good voice. Under different circumstances, I might have wanted to be seduced. Not today.

"That's nice. I'm the son of a dry goods and hardware store owner. Welcome to America."

"Very well." She shrugged. "You are not

making this easy on yourself. Seize him!" I expected to be rushed by the acolytes I'd seen, but four newcomers had joined them. I mentioned the gardeners looked pretty dirty. These four looked worse. I thought one looked like his face had a gangrenous patch. Smelled like it, too. Another was a woman, but although she was young, her eyes were filmed over with cataracts and her skin was waxen as well as pale. She held a bag in her hands. Newcomer three was also female, and her fingers had lost the flesh covering the tips, revealing bone. The final one didn't fit the pattern of most of the acolytes. He had a beard, was an older man, and wore regular but ragged clothes. He was bloated and had a pattern of dark veins on his nose.

Of course, this takes longer to describe than I took to notice them and quickly decide the way out wasn't through the crowd. There was a side door on the left, and I took a side leap, pivoted, ran a couple of steps, and then dropped to the wooden floor in a slide to dodge Gangrene's attempted tackle. I rose to my feet at the door and spun at the sound of footsteps to kick Vagrant in the gut hard enough to knock him on his tailbone. Fingertips had gotten tripped by one of the dopey acolytes. I couldn't see Cataracts, though. I turned the door handle, hoping I wasn't going into a dead end or worse, a closet.

The back of my neck prickled, like someone was watching me who I couldn't see, which was weird, because I was still facing the center of the room. I yanked the door open as hard and fast as I could, and heard a thud above me. Cataracts fell to the floor. She'd been lurking over the doorway, somehow. No time to ponder, I spun and ran. There was a hallway with a little stairwell to the left. Upstairs might be good for fighting, but not for flight. Forward would take me back toward the courtyard, closer to the main entrance but also a place to encounter more weirdos. The right door would possibly be an alternate path to the kitchen area, which should be connected to a back way for tradesmen to bring deliveries. You repurpose a flop hotel for a cult, you still have a hotel layout.

Right it was, and I came across what I can only call the Valhalla of cleaning supplies. It was far too big to be a broom closet, with a freight elevator right there to make it easy for maids to move carts of supplies up to the floors above or take trash down. A high window or maybe even a skylight somewhere allowed a lot of natural light in the room. Behind me, at the door, there were animal noises, huffing and hissing and growling. I looked back to see Cataracts and Gangrene looking in warily. "What the hell," I muttered. I started to wonder if the physical problems here extended beyond drugs to an outbreak of some bizarre form of leprosy. Completely illegal medical testing? I pushed carts behind me as I ran, turning order into disarray in the hope of slowing pursuit. My sweat came from fear at least as much as exertion. I grabbed a push broom to use as a makeshift defense.

Beyond Mop Valhalla was an array of dumbwaiters. If you don't live where there are tall buildings, those are basically mini elevators for moving things like trays of food or bags of laundry between floors with less work. This time, though, the doors were opening and what was being revealed was not dirty dishes or damp towels, but Fingertips unfolding herself from one to my left and Vagrant slithering out of another on my right. I had no idea how they could have gotten up to another floor and down the dumbwaiters so fast. I'm quick on my feet and it had really only been seconds since I left them behind.

There wasn't any time to worry about how they had got there, though. The only way to have time for anything now was to buy it. If I could drop the two who'd just come in, I should be able to get through the next door, maybe block it behind me. Vagrant seemed the more dangerous of the two, so I swung the broom in both hands and caught him on the side of the head with the wooden pole. That knocked him to the ground, but he didn't even shake his head to clear it. He just glared at me, snarled, and lunged for my throat.

Well, he might not think the floor was good enough for him, but it was good enough for me. I dropped and rolled to the side while his leap brought him smack into Fingertips, who was closer than I thought. She didn't take kindly to it and they started fighting each other, which suited me fine. I was back on my feet and going for the door when I was yanked suddenly backwards. I turned my head and found myself face to face with Gangrene. He was even uglier and more aromatic up close. His eyes were pretty red and whatever was wrong with him, I did not want to catch. I put the broom between us and tried to lever him off me. He didn't budge. Kneeing him didn't seem to faze him, either. Maybe it was true that leprosy hit there early.

Then everything went black. It wasn't that I lost consciousness. It was just that while I was trying to get loose from Gangrene, Cataracts had come alongside me and stuck the bag over my head. I was shoved against the door. If I hadn't been distracted by having the wind knocked out of me and my bones rattled, I'd admire the sturdy construction. I felt breath on my skin as I tried to wriggle free. Too many hands were gripping me too hard. One pushed my head back and that's when I heard Katie's voice again.

"NO!" she ordered like she was commanding dogs to 'leave it'. "You're not to harm him. Bind him and take him upstairs to the formal reception room. I'll handle him from there. You'll get your reward later."

They didn't simply tie my hands, or rather wrists, together. That's not such a bad situation. Forearms in concert can make a decent club, and given a minute or two alone, there's a good chance of getting loose or at least stepping through the loop backwards to get your arms in front so you can manipulate things. No. I was bound wrist and elbows, which were then tied down to my waist and thighs. I was sufficiently trussed to feel like I knew how a Thanksgiving turkey must feel, except for the sage and onion, and I sure hoped we left the area near the kitchen before someone thought about that.

"Soldier boy, will you walk, or shall I have them carry you?"

"Walk, please. I don't like the look of the help. But what am I supposed to do, put my hand on someone's shoulder to guide my way? Whoopsie, guess either the bag or the ropes need to go."

"Push him. He can figure out where to go or he can fall over." It had been worth a shot. The pushes weren't gentle, but they got me to the elevator. My feet itched to make a break for it, but without the ability to see or defend myself, trying to talk my way out was my best bet at this point and a show of cooperation on my part was a negotiation tactic. Just one floor up, I judged from acceleration cues, we stepped out (they stepped, I stumbled after another shove) and went down a hall (echoes are helpful). I was led around some furniture and shoved into a seat. The seat was upholstered, and seemed wide. A sofa, I surmised before seeing it.

SURE TO GIVE OFFENSE

When they took the bag off my head, the room couldn't have been more different than the spartan downstairs rooms. There was gold leaf on the old furniture. A crystal chandelier hung from the ceiling. Katie looked more at home here than I'd seen her before, relaxed as she sat in a chair watching me. I could hear noises behind me of people shuffling out of the room.

"You know something?" I figured I might as well start trying to talk my way out of this. "I haven't seen anything important. I mean, nothing illegal. I might suspect there's some kind of drug use going on, but that's just a guess, and even if you are doping people up, if it isn't on a list of restricted substances, the police can't do anything about it. No one is here against their will, uh, except me, and I think I can let that slide if you don't keep me here too long. I mean, you probably just want to talk with me about Eugene, right?"

"No, Mr. Jones, I do not want to talk with you about him. I want you to join us, at least for a while." She smiled slightly. I didn't find the smile reassuring.

"My mom would never forgive me; I was raised to be a good Catholic boy."

"That won't stand in the way. Not for long." She rose from her seat and began to walk over to me with a sway in her hips that belonged in a rhumba.

Just then, I heard the door open behind me, and smelled a pungent, organic odor. A rough voice snapped, "Yekaterina! I wish to see the intruder before you do anything."

"And I was starting to get curious about what she wanted to do. By the way, it's not intruder, it's investigator... and as I was telling your friend Katie, my investigation found nothing of interest."

Mr. Stinky turned to face me. When his eyes met mine, it felt like a punch to the gut. I'd never reacted to anyone that way, and I've looked into the eyes of killers and fanatics before. I didn't care how much force of personality he thought he had, though. I looked back at him even as I felt the beginnings of a headache. And my eyes were watering, but that might not have been his gaze, just his smell. "You will be quiet," he told me.

"I don't think so. I've got a reputation as a big

mouth and I can't just give it up now that I don't have a commanding officer to answer to."

The big man looked puzzled, which considerably lessened the drill-bore effect of his stare, especially when his eyes flicked over to Katie. She shrugged, a more complicated gesture than it needed to be and one that had me looking over at her, too. She was a lot easier on the eyes than her friend, even if she was every bit as evil.

"It's true," she said, "He is very mouthy. And apparently it isn't just me he can resist. Can I have him?" I didn't like that question at all. She continued, "I'm so hungry. I can't count how many times I've just wanted to rip Marshall's throat out, but I know we'll never take Russia back without him."

The hairs on the back of my neck were starting to rise. She didn't mean it metaphorically, I knew. Everything was starting to fall into place, not just the mention of taking back Russia, which gave me suspicions as to their funding, but the sheep-like followers, and the amazing speed and strength of the freaks. "You're a vampire. You both are." It didn't make sense. Things like that didn't exist. But I could practically see the bloodstains on their mouths in that moment.

Stinky walked over, grabbed me by the hair,

and looked into my eyes again. I was sweating fear, and kicked myself mentally for not keeping my mouth shut for once. It doesn't do to know too much when you're not in control of the situation. "This one may be special. Do you believe in vampires?"

"No. It's kid's stuff. Dracula is just a movie to take your dates to because they get scared and want to hold hands in the dark. But..."

"But you can sense our guilt."

"It's a policeman's instinct," I said.

"No," he said. "Most police are fools. They see guilt where they want to see it and let the most powerful, most guilty people go. You have a rare gift. I have it, too."

"I don't think we have anything in common," I growled.

"Of course we do. If nothing else, we are all sinners." His deep voice had taken a gentle tone, trying to be charming, ludicrous in the threatening circumstances. I found it more unsettling than Yekaterina's request. She wanted to drink my blood, and I didn't want that. But I couldn't understand what Stinky wanted and suspected it was worse.

"Me, I'm a choir boy. Well, I was. Church organist for a few years." I was running my mouth partly to keep from screaming and partly because every moment I kept talking, I wasn't being killed.

"Sneaking out of the house at night to go to a den of vice."

"A speakeasy! It wasn't that vice-filled. And I just went for the music and to earn a little cash doing odd jobs."

"And to be among the rich, beautiful women. Just like me."

His grip on my hair hadn't released and I was reaching a point of annoyance. Rather than being impressed by whatever kind of mind-reading magic trick this was, I was getting annoyed.

"Yeah, and you and Yekaterina are getting along so well. Maybe she wouldn't keep looking like she smelled something bad if you washed once in a while."

I guess that one stung, because his free hand moved in a blur and his fist hit my head like a baseball bat. *I'm probably getting a concussion,* I thought as my vision wobbled, *but not too bad of one. At least I know I'm concussed.* If I pushed his temper harder, he could kill me barehanded, with that much strength. I wondered if I should. I didn't want to end up undead. But I also didn't want to be dead at all. I had too much to do, most importantly to warn Eugene about "Katie" and tell

Clara she's right about the killings being done by the art thieves but that they are something worse than ordinary criminals. The neck wounds on the dock workers were explained now, if my theory was right, and really, Russians with a taste for blood and expensive things just made the connection to the initial case too obvious now. Even if I could just get to a phone unobserved for a few minutes, I might save lives.

I had to play along for a while. "Sorry. I must just be a little jealous and it's making me lose my manners." If you want to get a suspect to trust you, give a truth. "I am a sinner in that sense, women. The first time I went to confession after really getting into it with a girl, the priest refused to absolve me. He said I was obviously rejoicing instead of repenting. He was not wrong."

He laughed and (finally!) let go of my hair. Great, now I was even dizzier. "I like this one!" he told Yekaterina. "He has plenty of spirit to survive the transformation."

"We've had three failures so far here."

"If I can butt in... if you mean what I think you mean, isn't it four?" There had been four decaying attackers. Now that I knew undead was a possibility, it was obvious they were vampires. Whatever failure meant, it had to do with why those ones were rotting and acting like animals while Katie and Stinky could pass for human.

Katie shook her head. "You can't count the vagrant. He wasn't supposed to be turned. We arrive in new places hungry and take someone who won't be missed for our first feed. But he fought back. He *bit* Grigori!"

"The nerve!" I agreed cheerfully. No one ever sees their own hypocrisy, right? Now Stinky had a name, Grigori. "Say, if we're going to be on a first name basis, I'm Rafael, not The Intruder or This One."

"She and I are on a first name basis because we are intimate. To you, I am the holy man Rasputin."

I just managed to restrain my first reaction to that, which would have started with holy as well, but finished with something sure to give offense. The Mad Monk, adviser to the last Tsar, mystic healer and holder of a very dark reputation. "The guys who tried to kill you said it was almost impossible. You were poisoned, shot at point blank range, bludgeoned, and still alive when thrown into a river."

"Running water paralyzed me. When I was pulled out, people thought I was dead. I made sure they continued thinking that with a little hypnosis."

"But, technically, you were dead beforehand."

"Yes."

"When?"

"When I went on a pilgrimage to a monastery. Things happened there. I left a changed man."

"And you're looking to convert others."

"I want to bring all people closer to God."

"I can see that." From a twisted perspective, sure. Those who he murdered were reunited with their maker rather more quickly than they would have been in the normal course of events. His living followers must have believed they were having some kind of religious experience to be drawn in. "But—" I ran through my options mentally, very quickly. Don't argue theology with a fanatic. Don't mock the guy with the bad temper when you can't defend yourself. Don't show fear. "But you need to have a little faith that things will work out if you don't try and control everything. You see, I used to be a member of the NYPD. I still have friends. If I disappear, people are going to come around asking questions. You have your ways of managing questions, but the problem is, police are persistent. They come back. They ask questions of people you haven't even thought about."

"Destiny does not care about policemen. You do

not know how I have been spied on and investigated in the past."

"He has a point though, Grigori." I looked with some surprise over at Yekaterina. She was pretending to take little notice of me, fussing with her hair in a mirror on the wall. I could see her and Rasputin in it. I wondered how much I didn't really know about vampires as she went on. "If he was to be enthralled, we could just order him to act normally for a few days. He saw nothing of interest here. He can tell whoever hired him that Irene was getting ready to leave for Arizona to do missionary work and there's no use bothering her. And I shall be happy to make sure he does what he is supposed to. He can come back later, and you can turn him then." All the time, she was making eye contact with me in the reflection. "I should like to have him for a while. And if you want to be sure he experiences plenty of sin before he dies, that can certainly be done."

Before I could cast a vote, Rasputin came up behind her, moving fast and silent as she had done before. It wasn't a human way of moving and I felt a cold knot in my stomach at the unnaturalness of it all and my own position in the middle of it. He didn't attack her, at least not what one would normally call an attack. He folded his arm across her chest and pulled her to lean against him, speaking in her ear in Russian. She closed her eyes, but there was an unhappy tension in her face. I guessed he was telling her no. He looked over his shoulder at me. "If she takes control of you, you will lose your will, your sense of self. That would mean your spirit would be lost and you would be as mindless as the slaves who brought you here. That would never do." His hands stroked Yekaterina's skin, across her collarbones and up to her throat. She stood passively under his touch. I frowned. He kept speaking. "You are one of God's true Chosen, Rafael, destined for immortality and power, just like me. You will be my little brother."

"I've always liked being an only child," I replied.

I'd already been studying his movement patterns, so, fast as he could be, I caught the look in his eye and was off the couch and leapt sideways into a slide along the floor that took me under a desk and bought an extra second for me. That was enough time to get my weight on my feet, not to stand, but do a backflip. It sounded crazy, but agility and unpredictability were my only advantages, and my foot connected with his chin.

That had the effect of hurting him, and putting my landing off balance. I teetered and, once my back leg had caught up with the landing, I tried to swing and pivot into a roundhouse kick. Unfortunately, he'd had time, a flare of temper, and fast reflexes; with those on his side, he caught my leg and used it to swing me into a wall. For a moment I thought the wall was the floor, between the way I was pressed against it and the dizziness and disorientation that came right after impact. I was too stunned to move for a moment, and he closed in. An arm appeared in front of my face. It was bleeding. I smiled briefly, thinking I must have injured him without being able to recollect it, and then with horror, I tried to draw away.

He slammed his knee into my lower back and I howled with pain. That gave him the opportunity to stick his wrist in my mouth, jamming it open as his blood began to spill into my mouth. I squirmed, trying to get away, but his knee stayed in place in the small of my back and I couldn't move. I bared my teeth, just to try and get his foul blood out. It dripped out slower than it was flowing in, though, even if I tried to blow it out with my breath. Then he grabbed my nose so I couldn't breathe in at all.

I held out as long as I could, but with all the effort I'd been putting out, my body wanted oxygen so bad I couldn't resist. Reflexes older than thought took over and, desperate for air, I swallowed and then took what breath I could through my mouth. Once I'd done that, to my surprise, he stepped back, saying, "Children never want to take their medicine, just because it tastes bad."

Medicine? It was poison. I felt dirty inside. I dropped to my knees from pain and exhaustion, but I tried to vomit. I wanted to: the blood tasted sour, bitter, and earthy, and my stomach was churning. All I could manage was dry heaves. Rasputin laughed and started to walk away. "Katya, take him away and let him rest. He will survive his injuries, but I have plans for him tomorrow."

Then it was just me and Yekaterina. She put her arms under my shoulders and helped me to stand. I looked at her, surprised to see her frowning with concern. "You're the one who had me captured. But... you didn't mean for it to go this way. Are you going to help me?"

She frowned a little and shook her head. "It's too late already. But I hope you retain your mind. You might even be able to fight him then."

"What do you mean, it's too late? I'm still alive."

"But you will die. And if you die before he does, you will be one of us." Instead of guiding me to the sofa again, she steered me to the door and we began to walk down a hallway. So the sense of being contaminated inside wasn't just my imagination. Something dark and dreadful was starting to spread through my system.

"So I have to kill him before he kills me."

Her eyes widened as she looked me over again. I still had my arms secured behind my back. I must already have had bruises and abrasions starting from the first struggle, and falling on my face in the second couldn't have helped my appearance. "What makes you think you can?"

"I can't tell you unless I can trust you." To be honest, I didn't have a plan yet, just a general idea that since it didn't seem like he was going to kill me right away, I could maybe catch him during the day, when he'd be sleeping, and take him out when his strength and speed didn't matter. "I don't even know what to call you. Do you prefer Katie or Yekaterina?"

"I would like to hear you call me Princess." That should have been the snootiest thing she'd said yet, but her voice had been warm and maybe a little flirty.

"Princess, what you said about being free, and fighting him. He's got some hold over you, doesn't he? And you'd like him gone?"

"I didn't say that." She paused, "I'm not saying you're wrong, either. It's complicated. But I would like you to live. He wants you to be like us because you remind him of himself. But you remind me of someone very different." Her eyes got a soft, far-away look. "Someone nice. He was also reckless and insubordinate. I couldn't get him out of trouble. You, though..." She nodded. "Yes, I will give you a little help, to get yourself out of trouble."

"Got any exits that are unlocked and unguarded?"

She showed me into a room. It was spacious but barely furnished. "All are unlocked. We welcome unexpected visitors. Unguarded is harder. But... there is a basement exit out onto the street. I can see to it that that way is clear. The pantry behind the kitchen, or the main stairwell, are the ways down."

"Great. I can look for the pantry door while I'm getting a weapon."

"I... think the main stairwell would suit you better." She walked me over to a bed so I could sit on the edge of it.

"Okay." Maybe, maybe not. But I thought the pauses weren't her trying to trap me, but trying to walk a fine line between helping me and whatever kind of disloyalty would get her into trouble. If

Rasputin could really sense guilt, she was taking a risk. And she undid the knots on the rope binding me. I started rubbing my forearms, which tingled. I thought about how to ask her what I really needed to know and still let her dodge the responsibility for the answer. "Princess, if I do end up becoming a vampire, what would I be afraid of?"

She looked troubled for a moment, worried my will might be wavering, but then she got what I was getting at. "Oh, much of what you think. Sunlight, fire, beheading—" She began bustling about the room, pouring some water into a glass and bringing it to a table next to the bed.

"What about the stake thing?"

"It would work, but not if you had any opportunity to strike back. Easier to do with the failures. Their bodies have started to rot. But the flesh of an elite vampire is just as tough as that of the living, and the heart is very well protected, deep inside the chest."

"Keep yours protected, Princess," I told her. If I could kill Rasputin and get out, I'd find help to shut down the operation. But if she took off and stayed out of trouble, I wouldn't be interested in hunting her down. She had a personal reason for helping me, which gave me a personal reason for forgiving her. A personal reason wasn't necessarily a good one, but if we didn't listen to those impulses, we wouldn't have a sense of self that could transcend death. I had to meet kindness with kindness.

"It all depends," she said with a shrug. "I am going now," and she was indeed at the door. "You need to rest. But for now, remember John 3:16." The door locked behind her. The verse, of course, promised eternal life to the believer. But it also could refer to a room number on the third floor. I drank the water, and leaned back to give myself a chance to heal a little. I intended to stay awake, though, because I wasn't sure how bad the concussion was, nor what might happen if I wasn't watchful.

It was no good. There may have been something in the water, or maybe it came down to my injuries. I was out within minutes.

THE SCREAM CAME FROM DOZENS

When I awoke, I realized from the light outside that it was late in the afternoon. I muttered under my breath in disgust. Moving at noon would probably have been my best chance. But I'd been injured and the blood I'd been force-fed had probably been toxic in some way, so once I'd fallen asleep, I'd stayed that way. I told myself that just meant I needed to start quickly. I sat up and stretched. Only then did I see I was not alone in the room. Two figures stood in the shadows in the corner opposite the bed I was on. They had been watching me, and when they could see I'd spotted them, they began to simper and pose. One was Tammy, the Marshall Enterprises employee I hadn't found before. Since the other one was Cataracts, I guessed that Tammy was under the garden soil yesterday

This had to have something to do with Rasputin's sin-leads-to-salvation theory. However,

I did not find them seductive at all. I already knew Cataracts was basically a dangerous animal, and knowing Tammy had been turned was the source of a stomach-churning sense of rage and failure. Not being back in the U.S. long, I hadn't known her well, but I suspected we would have become friends, two Latinos going after professional work in the big city. Now, she hadn't started to decay yet, but it was clear her personality was gone.

With an effort I was able to put on a flirtatious smile. "Ladies, I can barely see you over there in the shadows. Why don't you move over there," I nodded to the heavily curtained windows, "and maybe put on a little show for me? Maybe you... fancy each other some, hmm? I'd like to see that."

What I really wanted to see was them squarely in front of the window. Once they'd gotten into position and were kissing each other, I sprang up, sprinted, and threw open the drapes. The afternoon sun streamed in. In the book for Dracula, he just sort of turned to ash in the sun, but in reality, flames began to dance on their skin almost instantly. They shrieked in panic as their filmy nightdresses caught on fire. Tammy tried to pat out the flames. Cataracts flailed about, then at the last moment, lunged toward me. I backed away, looking around for something to use as a weapon, but as I was doing so the crumbling into ash finally happened.

As much as a relief as that was, I still had a long way to go until safety. The windows had iron bars welded on, a crime deterrent by intention that meant my possible exits were limited. The curtain rod, though, I liked, because it also appeared to be made out of strong iron. I could lift it out of the brackets on the wall and had a decent weapon on me. If I ran into any humans ready for a fight, I could bop them with the side of it, and it had a pointy metal spiral bulb end that I could try stabbing with if I came across a vampire and had nothing better. It wasn't good enough for me to feel confident going after Rasputin with it, though.

There was one other thing to do at the window. I took out a handkerchief and wrote a note on it. "Eugene Marshall at Empire State bldg in danger. He needs to ditch Katie, disappear. Tell Clara Raf said to stop." It was the best I could do to warn them if I didn't make it. I tied the handkerchief around my wallet, hoping whoever found it would understand the contents were a reward for delivering the message, and I dropped it out the window to the street below.

The door was easy. It was still locked, but

since these amateurs hadn't bothered to search me, I had a few picks on me and got it open. Moving quickly but quietly, I searched for the stairwell. Whichever way I wanted to get to the basement, I needed to reach the ground floor first and the elevator was more of a risk. Even if Yekaterina betrayed me, at least stairs gave more options to run or fight.

When I found the stairs, I knew she'd been sincere. The fire kit was there. One portable extinguisher and one large fire axe. I gave it a practice swing. The head was weighty. All the better to behead with. I started on the stairs now, not going down, but up. Room 316 should be on the right.

There was another lock to pick, but I already had the technique pretty well down from the one for my room. Just like in the books, there was a coffin in the room, set up on a coffee table (a coffin table?). Good height for him to get into, but also a good height for me to behead him. I opened the lid. I was surprised at how young he looked with his face at rest. He must have been around my age when he really died. Keeping in mind I didn't want to die at age 35 myself, I picked up the axe and swung. It cut most of the way through his neck, but I hadn't thought about the edges of the coffin. The axe head struck his neck, but the shaft struck the coffin and stopped its motion with a loud clunk.

As it was, the blow would have killed anything mortal. His windpipe and major blood vessels were severed. Something like blood, but darker and thicker oozed out the edges of the wound. I drew back the axe, getting ready to strike again, knowing I shouldn't leave unless I was sure the job was complete.

Before I could begin my second stroke, his eyes flew open, looked around, then focused on me. Again, the power of his stare felt like something physical. I started to step back, then steadied my resolve. That's when he opened his mouth and screamed. His throat couldn't make the noise. The fluid welling from his neck frothed, but no sound came from the head in front of me. Instead, the scream came from dozens of voices, male and female, from every occupied floor of the building as all who were under his sway, the living and the dead, became his voice. I rushed to barricade the door, to give me time to deal with him. I looked back after sticking a chair under the know and gasped.

There was no longer anyone in the coffin. I didn't for an instant believe he had crumbled while

I had looked away. Instead, he must have changed form. A mist, perhaps, or bat. Forget barring the door. I was the hunted now, not the hunter. I flung away the chair, shouldered the axe, and headed back for the stairs. Outside, it was still daylight. Would still be daylight for perhaps half an hour. That was my one place of safety.

I took the stairs two at a time. I'd go out the main gate, I thought. To hell with worrying about it being guarded. Not when I've got a bloodied axe in my hands, who would stand in my way?

Innocent people who'd been bitten and enslaved. Thralls, as the vampires had called them. They would be called on to stop me, and I couldn't chop up a guy who couldn't help what side he was on. Basement it was. I feared meeting more undead, but at least I wouldn't have to fight my own conscience if I met them.

I still couldn't avoid all humans; some of the men were gathered on the first floor landing by the time I got there. But that was easy. The lead ones, coming up towards me, got kicked in the face and fell back on the rest like bowling pins while I vaulted, swinging around the arm rail, taking a toehold on the arm rail on the stairs to the basement, and clambering down while the thralls tried to sort themselves out.

I reached the basement. It was dim and cooler than the rest of the building. The landing there also had a door with a deadbolt I could set from the basement, avoiding pursuit, at least from humans. I wasn't sure about the vampires, and I wasn't sure I wasn't locking myself in with any. While the concrete floors weren't something anyone was likely buried under, it was a good place to avoid sunlight. I headed forward, looking around, when I found the way out, I sighed. This was one time I didn't want to be right.

Yekaterina stood between me and the stairs to the street. I stopped, cautious. "If you just want to say goodbye, I could send you a postcard." She'd helped me before, but that was before I'd really enraged Rasputin.

"You have squandered your chance, my darling," she said. Well, that was definitely her speaking.

"I'm not dead yet."

"But you will be. And he can be cruel. He will bring you pain and humiliation as punishment for raising your hand to him. I don't want you to suffer. It doesn't have to be terrible. The path to life beyond death can be a beautiful, blissful passage. Let me take you there, and then we can be together."

Oh, that was her speaking, for sure. She was as much a vampire as any of them and she may have held back earlier but my failure had given her all the excuse her hunger needed.

"I've killed a few vampires so far today. I almost killed Rasputin. I'm not giving up hope yet. If you don't want to be the next one to go to the next world, get out of my way." I shifted my hold on the axe, holding it clearly so she could see Rasputin's blood still glistening along the edge.

"A sleeping man and mindless animals. You've never fought a vampire for real. You're still standing."

I pulled back, ready to strike, and began to charge forward. Maybe she'd change her mind if she saw I was really willing to battle for my life. She waited until I drew close, then, as I swung the axe, she caught the head with surprising strength and pushed back against me. I tried to avoid the haft as it just about hit my stomach and got so off balance that her final shove sent me backwards and I landed on my butt at the base of the stairs. I sprang back to my feet. I'd managed to keep hold of the axe and held it ready as I stepped backwards while she walked toward me. Something brushed my leg and a glance showed me one of my suspenders had broken and was dangling. She sped up and I swung the axe again, this time, meeting no resistance. She turned into mist as it passed through her, unimpeded and harmless.

Her hands turned solid at my throat. I stifled an urge to scream, then realized she wasn't trying to choke me. She was just undoing the top button on my shirt. "Stop it!" I took one hand off the axe and swatted at her hands. Suddenly, there was a different feel there. I brushed at squeaky hair and then a bat flew away. I ducked behind some old barrels, trying to keep my eye on her. I heard someone running on the ground floor and I looked back at the main stairwell for a moment.

Then the bat dove into my hair. I reached up to grab it and got two soft hands instead. One slipped away and slapped my ear, but lightly. I tried to dodge out between two of the barrels but she suddenly shoved one into the other, trapping me. While I was squirming free, she leaned forward and patted my backside.

I was quite aware that the fight had become ridiculous to the point of embarrassment. She was right— a human was completely physically outmatched by the combination of speed, strength, and magic powers a vampire had. There was only one real way out of this. I moved back into the unobstructed floor space while she climbed over the barrels with a cat-like fluidity. "I get it. You're that much faster and stronger than me, and he'd be worse. You're also just playing, not really trying to hurt me." Although I'd have some bruises. "You want me to be willing. To see that what you're offering me is not such a bad thing. I can see that now." I dropped the axe. "But don't just bite me, okay. I want a real kiss first, Princess. I want to believe there's going to be a happy to this ever after."

Yekaterina smiled as she came to me. I had my hands in my pockets, still a little shy, and only raised them to hold her when she embraced me. The lock pick in my hand was a good nine inches long, hard steel, and more slender than any stiletto ever made. I kissed her, thinking of Clara as I did so to make the sensation more believable, to make sure I didn't draw away from cold lips. They turned out not to be all that cold and the kiss wasn't as difficult as the moment when I drew back my arm and then stuck the pick through her back and deep into her heart.

She stiffened, frozen in place. But as I suspected, such a tiny wound wasn't enough to destroy her. I left the pick there to hold her. "I'm really sorry, Princess, but even if I can't win this fight, I have to try. I wouldn't be me if I didn't do everything I could. But I have to get moving while there's still light out." I picked the axe back up and ran up the stairs to the street outside.

THOU SHALT NOT KILL

And there I was, a man with a busted suspender and a bloody axe, out on the streets of New York City. I didn't want to get arrested, so I'd need to have my driver's license and ditch the axe. But I wanted to protect myself, so I needed to stay armed. Before making a decision on the axe, I figured I'd see if my wallet was still in the alley I dropped it in.

I hesitated briefly. The sun still shone up the side of the building on the second floor windows and higher, but as the sun was getting lower, shadows of nearby buildings fell across the street. Shade was a risk. It was already obvious that vampires could be active by day, but the sun posed such a threat to them that their movements were limited. Act now, I decided, but as I started forward, a large shape dropped out of the building to the street.

A body. I ran up to investigate. Her wrists had

been slit. It might look like she'd tried to commit suicide that way, then jumped out the window, if you weren't thinking about how little blood showed at the cuts. Like they'd been licked clean as the blood stopped running. I looked up. Two thralls stood on either side of the window, watching me without real interest. I was just there, like the body they'd been told to throw out.

Then a voice came from further back in the room. A powerful, deep voice I'd rather never hear again. "Little brother, this is on you. When one of us is injured, we need to feed to heal. I'll be well enough to come bring you home... in another drink or two!" One of the thralls at the window disappeared with a squeaky yelp, pulled into the darkness of the room.

I ran. Chances were the wallet was gone and I didn't need to navigate the shadowed street under eyes he might be able to see through. I wasn't sure where I was headed yet. I couldn't go directly to Eugene. He had been their original target and Yekaterina knew I was connected to him. I could call, though. I shouldn't go home, either, because my apartment was just over my office which was on my business card, which they'd have because of Irene. I could make a call from a pay phone. Afterwards, I'd get in my car and start driving.

Maybe all the way to Washington, D.C.— I could find Clara and either get her to believe what was going on, or join Interpol myself and maybe take over the case and get her reassigned.

I found a phone booth across the street from where I'd left my car. I dialed Eugene's apartment and got a busy signal. I tried his office number and got his answering service. Well, it was worth a shot. I told them Major Jones had to meet with Mr. Marshall urgently, at the Capitol Building in Washington, D.C., tomorrow at 10 AM. It was a top secret matter and he was to bring no one with him nor tell any of his social circle. His office, of course, had to be told something because it was business, but he was to be discreet. He might not even get the message, I knew, but if he did, his sense of duty should get him out of their clutches for a while and I could meet him to warn him in person if I made it there.

The sun was setting. Pink sky showed around the edges of buildings, but the streets were pretty much all shadowed now. I jaywalked to my car, but when I got there, I saw the tires were shredded. So much for driving to safety. Heart pounding in my chest, I prayed it had been petty vandals and headed down the street. In a way, I just had to make it through the night. Then I'd have more options while they were pinned down. We'd passed the spring equinox so day was longer than night, giving me a time advantage.

Oh, the things I was telling myself to keep my spirits up. I knew it was whistling in the dark, but if I panicked or despaired, I'd stop thinking of tricks. Get lost in a crowd. Find an all-night deli with garlic all over the doors and windows. I turned down a couple of streets randomly. It was a big city. One man could be hidden for a long time if he wanted to be. I started to feel legitimately optimistic for the short term, before I was thrown into the wall of a building. I mean literally picked up from behind and thrown, hitting about eight feet up the wall and rebounding before falling to the ground. At least I landed on my feet. I spun around, back to the wall, and looked both ways along the sidewalk, seeing nothing but ordinary looking people.

It had surely been Rasputin. I couldn't tell where he was, so I darted across the street, looking hastily around as I avoided a car. A little old man suddenly turned into a bat and fluttered across after me. For a moment, I thought there were more vampires than I'd known of. Then he went back to his usual form in front of me. If I didn't recognize him with his drastically shortened beard, I'd know him by his smell.

"Thou shalt not kill, little brother. You've been a very naughty boy."

"I'm not so sure that commandment is meant to apply to undead." I hefted the axe. "Care to test whose side God wants to take?"

"I already know. It is you who need spiritual growth. Repentance is the only path to salvation. I give you some time to think on it more, little brother. But not much more time."

He dissolved into mist slowly. I began to run again. Trying to hide in a crowd would be no good. He could look any way he chose, apparently, so any stranger might turn out to be my enemy. A delivery truck was passing, one with a running board and I stepped up and grabbed on. The driver didn't seem to care and I was able to ride as far as a dock near the Brooklyn Bridge where the driver stopped to take on some crates. I waved a thank you as I took off toward the bridge.

I seemed to remember that vampires were supposed to have trouble crossing water. If I was lucky, I'd be out of his reach just by getting on the bridge. If I wasn't lucky, I'd just set myself on a linear path where there was little chance of dodging and the ability to fly would be a distinct advantage. There were no safe bets to play at this point. I ran; it couldn't hurt to get as much distance behind me as possible. I swerved my path to keep clear of other pedestrians. Mostly to make sure they didn't get alarmed by me or in the way of an attack on me, but also some because I didn't want to be within reach of a disguised Rasputin.

All seemed normal. The traffic ran noisily a bit below the pedestrian way. The view over the water was beautiful, the last crimson light of the sky giving way to indigo night. A moment later, it seemed to me to look like a dark robe covering up spilled blood and I looked away from the water and back to the cars going by. One black sedan seemed to have an unusually lumpy roof. Dark robes, dark hair, I knew what he was going to do before the lump turned into a leaping vampire.

So I swung the axe. Caught his arm, but as it entered his flesh, he turned, deflecting the blow from his body. I hurt him, at least. His cry of pain and shock restored some confidence. He was powerful, but not invincible. His hand went to his wound, then he held up the smear of blood for me to see.

He grinned. "You've already developed a taste for it, eh, little brother?" He laughed as I backed away. "But you mustn't be greedy. It is someone else's turn this time. Katya would like to taste you,

I know, but I am cross with her. She tried to take you without my permission, didn't she? And then she was stupid. Or shall we say you were clever? I can be generous. You were clever."

My swing of the axe, as I swerved around a post to be somewhat sheltered from him, passed right through him as he went to mist and back. "But not that clever. You understand, don't you? You will be one of us. It is your destiny."

I swung again, but this time, he grabbed the shaft of the axe and stopped it. I could feel the impact shock through my arms, and before I could decide to let go or try to yank it back, he had lunged forward and wrapped his free hand around my throat. He started to choke me and I desperately tried to free myself, dropping the axe so I could use my hands to try to loosen his grip.

He pushed me over to the edge of the bridge, then, taking both hands, he lifted me over the railing. As I dangled in his grip, I looked down at the dark, crashing waves under the bridge. A fall from this height ran a serious risk of fatality. But if not, the currents might carry me to safety. "There sure is a lot of water down there," I said. "I wonder if there's enough to wash your stench off of me."

He let go. The problem is, I couldn't. My basic

survival instincts made me grab on to the bridge as I fell. Even though I'd thought falling wasn't as bad as having him kill me, my hands wanted to survive as long as possible and refused to release their grip.

Before I could regain control, as I looked down at the water, Rasputin's long hand closed around my wrist. "Not like that, little brother." He then not only pulled me up, but held me over his head. I was trying to reorient myself when he threw me out into traffic. I went limp and rolled, hurting all over and wondering when the impact would come. But I lucked out, no one crushed me and I came to a halt in the middle of a lane, not daring to move as the undercarriages passed over me. Well, for someone trying to be motionless, I was probably shaking harder than a shimmy.

A car came to a stop above, as I stayed as flat as I could. I nervously opened one eye as a man's voice spoke above the cars honking in annoyance as they passed. "Hey, are you alive down there?" I saw an older man, a little beefy in the face, peering at me in the shadow.

"For now."

"Can you move?"

"It seemed safer not to until now." I started to belly crawl toward him. Drivers were swerving around us, but they didn't like it and some rude words were shouted as they passed.

"You need a ride to the hospital?"

"No, I wasn't hurt too bad." And I didn't want to end up in Bellevue.

"Police? I saw the guy push you." I could hear his voice drop a little as he said push. He'd seen me thrown, but pushing was easier to believe.

"Sounds like a good idea." I finished pulling myself out from under the car and got to my feet. He started to get back in the car, but left his door open until I was squarely behind the vehicle and headed to the other side, to keep traffic steering away.

"Is there someone after you?"

"Yeah. It's a long and weird story." I wasn't moving fast, but I got into the passenger seat and he started up the engine again.

I was hurting pretty bad and he could see it. "You're sure about the hospital?"

"It's all bruises."

"You got lucky, I guess," he said. "You want to tell me the story?"

"Not really. Some of the bruises are on my ribs." I could still feel tightness in my throat from the near strangulation, too.

He nodded. "I know how that is. Try and keep

your breathing shallow. My name's Joe." I took another look at Joe. He had a kindly face, but a cauliflower ear, calloused hands, and a number of scars showed he probably did know what he was talking about.

There was another traffic slowdown near the end of the bridge. It looked like there had been some kind of accident. A car was flipped on its side near the exit and a cop was directing traffic around it. I felt a moment of nostalgia seeing the uniform. I hadn't done that kind of basic work in a long time, but the simplicity of it was something I missed just at that moment. That's why I found myself looking back at the traffic cop after we passed him, in the side mirror. The mirror revealed the true identity of the figure. I shuddered and slumped down in my seat.

"The police can't keep me safe." I explained, "That was him, posing as a cop. He must have marked us, too. Please, just drop me off in a few blocks, and then take off as fast as you can. I didn't mean to get you involved in this."

"You sure?"

I nodded. My options were looking worse, but I wasn't going to drag a decent man down with me.

He pulled over and pointed to the back seat. "I'm a union man. I've got plenty of gear intended for defense. Take your pick."

"I don't suppose you have a fire axe."

"Sure do. Some bosses last month threatened to burn down a warehouse with some guys inside shutting it down through a sit in. Had to make sure we could protect them. Check the yellow toolbox."

There it was, smaller than the hotel version, but it might be easier to use. I grabbed an awl, too. "Thanks for everything, Joe. Stay safe."

The Manhattan streets were pretty well lit, but that didn't mean much. He'd attacked me on the bridge where people could see. I'd ruled out the police for safety because seeing him playing traffic cop— he'd probably flipped the car to give him an excuse— reminded me I'd told him I had been on the force. Hospitals were too obvious, given that he must know I was injured. As someone used to looking for missing persons, I knew some places were just too easy to check.

I turned left. Suddenly, where I should go was obvious. I wasn't too far from The Church of Our Lady of Victory. It had still smelled new when I went there some weeks ago when I got back from Europe, but it was as sacred as any ancient cathedral. Maybe more so, in my heart, because it was, in part, a memorial to men who'd served with me. It was also a celebration of the triumph of good over evil. If I could make it there, I could wait until dawn. The priests might not believe what I had been through, but they wouldn't turn away a veteran seeking refuge from demons, even ones in his head.

Once I knew where I was going, I sprinted all out. Maybe I'd even find another way to escape the corruption of the vampire's blood inside of me. God couldn't possibly let me be turned into a monster. Sure, in *Dracula*, Mina had been burnt by the Eucharist after she was tainted with vampire blood, but clearly Stoker hadn't known everything. Just because Rasputin was madder than a rabid raccoon didn't mean he was wrong about seeking salvation.

The cross on the wall before the alcove with the stained glass on the doors reassured me. I'd made it. He'd have to wait for another night, surely, but I worried about Eugene. I slid into a pew to rest for a few minutes, out of breath and throbbing with pain. I wished I had my rosary with me, but it had seemed a bad idea to take into a cult. I said a few prayers anyway. I needed all the help I could get, and it calmed me while I thought of what to say when I spoke to a priest. I wanted communion, or something to drive the darkness of the vampire blood out of me, even if it would be dangerous. I could also use practical help if it were possible. There must be a phone on the premises, for instance, so I could try to get hold of my friends again.

At last, I felt I knew how to broach the topic. The confessionals were in back, underneath a balcony where the organ was. I pocketed the awl, but left the axe on the pew. It wasn't like I'd need it in here and if I did sound crazy I didn't want the priest to feel threatened. Once back there, there was nothing to do but pray some more while I waited for the priest to come. There was probably a buzzer or light that told them when someone came outside of the usual service hours, what with this place being so modern. This was an age of technological miracles and wonders, even if I'd come for the traditional kind.

There was a sound on the other side of the confessional. The priest must have entered. I took a deep breath, having given some thought to what I needed to say. "Forgive me, Father, for I have committed the sin of pride. I took on a fight too big, one I can't win on my own. I need help. Other people need help, too. If you have a phone in the church, maybe I can use it, but no one who enters here should leave until morning. I don't know if you take the idea of the forces of darkness literally, but they're real, and they may have followed me here. I'm sorry, Father. I've tried not to put anyone else at risk, but if I don't get help, I could become a danger to others myself. Please, please understand. I've been corrupted, but surely Christ can make me clean again."

I stopped and listened. "At last you repent. Maybe not quite right, but it is good enough. It is time for you to be forgiven and be granted eternal salvation."

Need I say whose voice it was? I had started to lunge for the door before his hands broke through the thin wall between us, grasping at me. He only got hold of my shirt, and with my adrenaline surging, I broke loose as the fabric tore.

I ran up the aisle between the pews. Maybe holy water from the font would help even though he'd managed to enter the church itself. Or the crucifix over the altar. Once I'd accelerated, I slid along the ballroom-smooth floor to the very stairs leading to the altar. I put a foot on the stair as I rose, stretching forward as if pleading to Christ on the cross to save me. But a figure attached to a wall doesn't make much of a weapon, so I pivoted even as I did so and sprinted to the font with the holy water while Rasputin overshot where I'd been and tackled the altar.

He howled. A bit of smoke arose, but he straightened up, red marks on his face and hands and raised those hands towards the crucifix, his face alight with religious ecstasy. "Yes! Let me feel the pain of sacrifice with you. We who are holy can endure it and cleanse the sins of man!"

I muttered, "There's nothing holy about anything this guy does, Lord. Please help me. I can't become a monster like him." I scooped up the holy water and drank it, hoping it would have some effect. My hands tingled like when you stretch a leg that's gone to sleep under you, and it hit my mouth and throat like pure alcohol. My stomach started to feel a powerful burning, but before I could tell if the final effect would be damage or cure, Rasputin had taken hold of me by my hair again. I splashed him with the holy water and had the satisfaction of seeing his skin blister, melting slightly where he was hit. He didn't stop, though. He forced my head back, and his fangs sunk into my throat.

It hurt. Movies and books never really convey that, the need to scream and the pressure of the bite closing your larynx shut. The tearing of flesh as he moved his head. And something else, the darkness in my blood, his blood in me, responding to him, pushing my own blood to him and filling me with an aching, cold anger. Every beat of my heart seemed to slow as the light around me dimmed. Yet one light still seemed to shine above me, bright in the distance, and just before I died, I heard a voice in the room saying, "You! Stop what you're doing! You do not belong here."

Left the miracle a bit late, was my final thought.

TO INVESTIGATE MY OWN DEATH

I woke up. It was cold and dark, and I didn't like the smell of the place. It had the scent of carbolic acid, of decay, and of old, stale blood. I was frightened. I was also more than a little confused. Hadn't I... hadn't I died? I had fallen unconscious, at least, and there was no reason to think he'd have spared me. I started to sit up and hit my head on something. I felt around. There was a flat surface above. Very carefully, I slid my hands around the side. I was on a tray, on a wire shelf. I was on a shelf in a morgue refrigerator. I still had clothes on. I guess they hadn't done an autopsy on me yet. Maybe they didn't need to. The injuries I came in with must have been pretty obvious. Besides which, if they were waiting for someone to identify the body, it would go better if I was more or less intact. They'd probably even have a copy of the initial police report. I should try and get hold of that.

I realized I was still thinking like a detective. That was a good thing. If I was undead, at least I wasn't one of those mindless ones. I knew who I was and what I needed to do: get out of here and stop the bad guys. I paused a moment. What if there was some kind of miracle or mistake? I ran my tongue over my teeth. Oh, I was definitely a vampire. But since the worst had happened, I had nothing left to lose.

I heard footsteps approach, just one pair. That was probably good, but I remember Yekaterina and Rasputin were both light on their feet. I couldn't be sure they weren't looking for me. One heartbeat, audible just after the footsteps. Again, could I be sure the person was alone? It didn't matter, I decided. Either way, I needed to be ready to get out.

When the door swung open, I launched myself forward, pushing against the sides of the unit for acceleration. I head butted the attendant on his chest, and ended up having to tumble over a body on a gurney. No one else in sight— he was just getting ready to put away another stiff. As I rose to my feet, I wondered if I was actually just really concussed. The morgue attendant had a kind of aura around him, mostly white and yellow lights, with a few ribbons of green and pink. I took a step closer and more of the light turned green.

"Oh, my God, mister!" he said. 'Someone's made a terrible mistake!"

I paused. "Am I still alive?" I wanted to believe it so bad I almost forgot that I had fangs. But as I moved closer to him, the heartbeat demanded my attention and my mouth began to water. "I'm sorry about this," I told him. And I sincerely was sorry, as I brought my fist around to catch him with a stunning punch. Didn't need a cosh for that anymore. I eased him to a sitting position, leaning against the metal door. The aura around him dimmed a little, but not much. I had to feed.

And on the gurney, there was someone who didn't need their blood anymore. Without going into the details, I got enough that the poor worker on the floor wasn't a temptation anymore. Found a few vials that had been taken for testing and downed them, too. Then I collected my things. I'd been around morgues enough to know where to look for personal effects of unidentified bodies and where to find the morgue copy of the police report. I checked myself out in the restroom mirror before leaving the building. I didn't need the reflection to know I still had my sense of self, but I needed to know if I would draw attention to myself. No— someone had washed the injuries while they were still there, I guess, and the bite marks had healed up. There was a lot of blood on my shirt, though. Figured Rasputin would be a messy eater. The guy had no class.

I mentally issued another apology to the morgue worker, and though I left what was in the coat pockets behind, I took a coat that was hanging on a hook on the wall. It covered up the bloodstains and other damage to my clothing. Besides, I couldn't shake the feeling of being cold. It was night, of course, but when I left the building, the streets were still crowded and would continue that way for hours. This was the city that never sleeps and ends up tossing and turning if it tries.

Everywhere I went, I saw that flickering aura around people. Some were brighter than others, some had different colors. A few people, some of the older ones and some of the bums, had dull gray sections. I looked at my own arms as I walked. What faint aura existed was mostly gray, but amid them, flickers of light and color would bloom. There was also something I hadn't seen on anyone else; ropy flares of something black and sticky looking. I was pretty sure that was what made me a vampire. It made me think of the feeling of Rasputin's blood in my system, dark and ominous. I wondered what the other auras meant.

I had picked my pocket change up with my other personal effects, so I took the subway. Time mattered, for other people at least. Once I had a seat, I pulled out the police report and went through it. I might know the lead-up, but I still wanted to investigate my own death. I didn't have ID on me when I died because of deliberately dropping my wallet, but you might expect the Catholic clergy to want to do something when a guy is killed by a vampire on their turf. For that matter, it seemed weird that Rasputin had just left me.

Going over the report, it turned out I hadn't been found in the church, but blocks away. In fact, on the Manhattan side of the Brooklyn Bridge. A policeman who had been summoned to the site of an overturned vehicle accident had spotted a tall, bearded man carrying a body. He'd radioed for backup while making his approach and the suspect had gone down a dead end alley and disappeared. I had been dropped— I guess even with vampire strength, you can't lift a grown man with itty-bitty bat wings. The cop on the case hadn't been on the job long enough to recognize me. I'd been sent to the coroner, but the complete autopsy hadn't been done. Initial case notes mentioned extensive, diffuse contusions and abrasions, and possible fractures consistent with accidental injury. "Or getting deliberately thrown off a bridge into traffic," I muttered. The body had been mauled by a large animal, possibly the final cause of death. "Damn right, and he was a vicious beast!"

I looked up and noticed some of the people in the car eyeing me. I gave a tight-lipped smile to indicate it was okay, I was just reading something upsetting. I wasn't some weirdo they needed to worry about. Except that was a lie; I was the most dangerous thing most of them would meet that night, and maybe the most dangerous thing they'd meet in their lives. The blood at the morgue wasn't really sufficient. Not for recovering after having my own drained. I put the report away, closing my eyes to shut out the attractive glow of the other passengers' auras. There was no way to shut out their heartbeats or their scent, but the temptations weren't stronger than my desire not to be a monster. If I didn't kill anyone, Rasputin wouldn't really win.

I went straight home and locked the door behind me. I checked my messages. Clara had left a request for me during the day, for me to meet her for lunch tomorrow. I phoned Clara's D.C. hotel. She'd checked out. I called the one she'd been staying at here in New York. The least I could do was let her know how things stood. I'd handle the Russians, but she needed to stay away from them and from me.

"Hello?" she answered. "Can I not be off the clock for an evening? Do you have any idea what time it is here?"

"We're in the same time zone. It's me, Raf. Listen. I won't be able to meet up with you tomorrow. Or at all. I'm a dead man now. And you should drop the Russian art theft case. It's too dangerous. I'll take care of it from here. But there's one thing. Eugene Marshall's in danger. Can you watch him?" I set the phone back down before I had to answer questions that I couldn't. My head was in a muddle over what to do about this existence, but I knew that at least that much I had to do— take down Rasputin and any other vampires that posed a danger to people here.

I figured the first thing to do was to arm myself appropriately. I wasn't exactly an expert on vampire slaying, although I might have the most experience of anyone locally. Wooden stakes were still supposed to be a reliable weapon if you put it in their hearts and this time I'd have the strength to do it. So I went up to my apartment, broke a chair at the kitchen table and started to whittle. It might not be the most effective approach, but like I said, I was muddle-headed with emotion. A few days ago, everything had been going right for me. Now I wasn't even human. Hunger distracted me, too. I set down the knife and half-finished stakes and went through my cupboards looking for something. The oversized canines would get in the way of chewing— I'd cut up the inside of my lower lip already, and the taste of my own blood wasn't appeasing me. I settled for some beef broth, a soft cheese, and applesauce. The broth was all right, but I had trouble eating the cheese or applesauce without gagging. I managed a few bites of each, for a loose interpretation of the word bite, but they didn't seem to be sitting well in my stomach, either. This wasn't good. I couldn't see myself on a diet of blood, but I had to have something. Hunger could make people do strange things, and if I couldn't find an adequate substitute, I'd have to find a safe source of blood or I'd end up losing control. I was about to see if the milk in the icebox was still drinkable when my phone rang.

I picked up before the second ring ended. Only after I'd done so did I realize I hadn't decided if I should let anyone know I was here. On the other end was Clara. Of course.

"You idiot," she said by way of greeting. "How

can I keep an eye on Eugene if he's left and no one knows where he went?"

"I stood you up, sort of, so I'll take the idiot bit, but I didn't know he was gone. Damn! Yekaterina must have got him."

"Who?"

"Katie. She's actually one of our Russians. She may not be a thief. She might have a claim to those treasures— I think she's an actual princess— but we still need to stop her and—" I took a deep breath. "Wait there for me. I'll nose around and see if I can't find a lead on where they are headed. I've got a bad feeling they'll be taking him out of the country."

She sounded more serious now. "You think he's in danger, don't you? I'll make some more phone calls. I may be able to have them delayed. Passport problem, that kind of thing."

"There will be another guy with them, six foot four, dark hair, crazy eyes, stringy beard. Let your people know to handle it in a way that doesn't alarm him. He's extremely dangerous."

W. I. T. C. H. HUNTERS

On the way there, I made up my mind to tell her everything. She had to know exactly what risks she was taking with them... and with me. Luckily, I knew Eugene had been working on special blood-clotting bandage material as well as the stain-resistant cloth I'd seen Diane working on, and so I went into his lab first and found a couple of bottles of blood for testing in an icebox. I had opened one and started to drink when I heard a throat being cleared. I turned to see Clara watching me. She looked annoyed, and I must have been shame-faced because I felt it. Her expression melted into concern in seconds. "My God," she said, "then you weren't using a figure of speech, were you?"

"No. I really am a dead man. I woke up in the morgue this evening and called you as soon as I could." She, on the other hand, was so very much alive. Her aura was a radiant mix of white, rose, and gold that made me want to touch it, to touch her, to wrap myself in that light and feel alive again for a little while. She was the most beautiful person I'd ever seen.

"I'm so sorry."

She meant it. There was worry on her face, but on my behalf. Maybe she was also saying she was sorry for her anger, now that she knew I what I was trying to cope with. I finished the pint, though I turned away to do it. Then I told her, "It changes things, but it doesn't change the job we have to do. The bad guys are just a little trickier to deal with, and we need to end them, not just arrest them. Yekaterina and Rasputin— yeah, that Rasputin, the Mad Monk— want Eugene's genius to help them take over Russia. If they're leaving, they're going to want to cover their tracks again, so I also have to go to their headquarters, evacuate the living, and kill the remaining dead properly."

"I take it that dead means vampires, or are we dealing with some other form of undead?"

"Vampires. You're taking this all a little too much in stride."

"I lied about not being in covert ops. Wartime Intelligence, Tactical Cryptoid and Heritage Hunters."

The first part of what she said had been

obvious, but the second threw me for a loop. "WITCH Hunters?"

"Well, it's a catchy acronym, but any witches involved were generally on our side. With the Nazis having an interest in the occult, we had to have our own lines of inquiry. I never actually met a vampire before, but I do have some training in dealing with them."

"Sounds useful."

"Some of it."

"Only some?"

She did an imitation of a gruff-voiced trainer, apparently Scottish. "If the locals tell you not to go to the castle after dark, do not go up to the goddamn castle after dark! If they want to put up garlic around the windows, learn to love the smell of garlic."

"Skip to offensive tactics."

"There's the 'Stoker tricks': destroy the heart beyond healing, decapitation, sunlight, and holy objects. There are also some theoretical weapons, things that ought to work but haven't been sufficiently field tested, such as a shotgun full of rock salt, or something like a focused floodlight."

"Uh-huh. Did you have anyone produce prototypes for any of these theoretical weapons?"

She smiled. "I have some very good news..."

We found the modified floodlight at the back of a low cabinet. There was another invention piled in with it, a series of radios and a complicated turntable with a record on it etched into steel. I handed those to Clara. "We're taking these along."

"What for?"

"Getting any enthralled humans to evacuate the building. It's a sonic crowd retreat, evacuation, and withdrawal encouragement device."

"That acronym won't work well in the press," she mentioned after mulling over the name for a moment.

I was hauling the floodlight out as she spoke. Curved mirrored panels wrapped around the huge bulb. A set of lenses could be snapped into place in front of it. It weighed more than I did and the power cables weren't finished. If we had Eugene, he'd know exactly how to set it up, but I had to say, "This is too complicated for me to use, and it's cumbersome. I could carry it, but if I did, I don't see how we could power it."

"Bring it along and put it in the car, I might be able to improvise if we need it."

"Can you improvise a flamethrower, too? Fire's pretty effective."

"There should be some welding supplies around here, so I think so. Not a lot of distance, unless we find one ready to go, but something very hot and very reliable up close. I'd still like to find the salt shotgun."

"Can you explain that one to me? I don't understand how that would help at all." While we talked, we started going through the drawers that ran through the 'devices' section of the lab.

"Well, most of the known ways to kill or incapacitate a vampire either use religious power or things that destroy magic."

"Magic is something that can be destroyed?"

"Oh, yes. Sometimes one finds a harmful object, and it can be purified by exposing it to sunlight for three days or dropped into running water. Putting it in a jar of salt will also do the trick, and salt is used in summoning circles and exorcism to control energies."

"Dropped into running water. Would that kill a vampire?"

"Possibly, possibly not. It would definitely incapacitate it and that might suffice. A helpless vampire could be dispatched if it could be reached, and if it was in the ocean, well, it would be meat for sharks and crabs like any other corpse." Her tone was dispassionate.

"I think I'm more afraid of you than you are of me," I said.

"Of course you are," she eyed me. "You're not a killer, as I clearly recall."

"I'm not the same as I was a few days ago."

"Really? Has that actually changed? Have you killed anyone?"

"No. Well, a couple of vampires. No humans. I've thought about it, though."

"Who hasn't? Say, I think I've found our weapons! There's some things here I didn't expect, too." She pulled a box out and put it on the countertop. I came over to see. There was more than one type of firearm: a shotgun, hand gun, and even a musket, as well as several different types of load and a notepad describing all details. There were balls for the musket made of salt, wood, and a metal one. I picked up the wood one. It was carved all over. When I looked closely, it was inscribed in Latin.

"It's the prayer for the dead," I told her.

"It doesn't bother you?"

"Of course not."

"What about this?" She dropped something else into my hand. It was a bullet for the handgun. Another wooden piece, set in a low-powder cartridge, and it had crosses around it and a Star of David across the top.

"Huh. No. Does that mean these won't work?"

"Lodge that in the heart and it will do fine. The low powder charge means you should fire at close range for accuracy, but the bullet should stop inside the body. What I think I'm noticing, Rafael, has nothing to do with the weapons, but rather, with you."

"I'm not that spec—"

She slammed the metal musket ball against the counter and it activated something. Holes opened around the surface and water sprayed out. "How do you feel?"

"Damp."

"That's holy water."

"No. Holy water burns vampires like acid. He must have made a dummy prototype."

"Does that sound like Eugene to you?"

"No. He'd give you one you could test fully. Oh, God." I took a seat on a stool. "I saw what holy water did to Rasputin. I could tell it was fighting the corruption when I drank it."

"You *drank* holy water?!"

"Yes. I thought maybe—" I paused, "I didn't want to become this."

"Tell me everything while we load up," she requested. So I did. She took the shotgun and the hand gun, I would have liked to have the pistol myself, but I could fight the monsters close up and she couldn't, so she needed good, reliable arms. I had the stake I'd carved, and the welding equipment was easy for me to carry. I took the musket, too, although I thought trying to load it in the field would be inefficient. Better, there were cutting tools in the lab and a few pointy files and awls long enough to do a little cardiac exploration. I gave one of those to her. I didn't expect any other vampires to get close enough to her for it to matter. Me, though, I wanted her to have something in case I started to act on any of the ideas I couldn't keep out of my head.

And those ideas did keep shadowing me. Her aura was bright, her neck was graceful, and my improved senses gave me a reminder of how it had felt making out with her every time I caught her scent or heard her breathe. I didn't want to hurt her, but I wanted her.

"Grab some more blood," she told me before we left the lab.

"Huh?" Had she been picking up my thoughts? I didn't want her to know about the temptation I felt, because I was ashamed of it. It was one thing to want something fun and good for both of us, but not to be fantasizing about drinking her blood, or worse, changing her, too.

"You said Rasputin needed to feed after he'd

been injured. We're going into a fight, so we should have something on hand in case you get hurt. You're probably barely getting by as it is. You must have lost over two quarts when you were killed. Have you had that much since then?"

"No." I was a little relieved to have the math laid out for me. I was still craving the stuff because I hadn't even replaced what I'd lost, in a sense, although it couldn't work as directly as that. I drank some more before we headed out and felt like we were both safer for it.

FIRE AND ACID

We pulled up to the home of the Order of Repentance, soon to be a smoking ruin, in all likelihood, if we didn't take action. It was cold-hearted in the extreme, but it had certainly covered their tracks in San Francisco. They would want to leave neither "failures", as they called the animalistic vampires, nor the thralls who would, Clara concurred, recover with time and distance from the vampires and serve as witnesses to some of their activities.

First thing we did was set up the sonic dispersal equipment around the building. It looked like an innocent enough activity, simply setting up radios, so anyone in the area wouldn't be alarmed and get involved or involve the police. Those who didn't know about vampires would be at risk if they came too close to the place. More importantly, we were hopeful the sensory reaction would override any orders the thralls had been given to stay behind. Once everything was set up— the gramophone and transmitter powered by the car battery— we put in earplugs ourselves and started the player.

It felt like fire and acid running through my skull. I don't remember falling, but by the time Clara turned off the record I was on the pavement, on my side, curled up with my arms trying to protect my head. I lifted my face and through blurred vision, I could see that she was saying something to me because her lips were moving, but I couldn't hear. I took out the earplugs, and caught, "I asked what happened?"

"I don't know, exactly. The sound…"

"Good Lord, I should have thought of that. You and the rest of the vampires will have hearing like bats, and whatever ultrasonic cacophony he created to subconsciously irritate humans is completely audible to you. And apparently incapacitating. I heard more screams than yours, so I think those failures should be at least as vulnerable as you are to this little device, but… I think you'd best get well away before I turn it on again. Take five minutes to get clear, I'll turn it on for fifteen. Then you get back here just as fast as you can."

"But you'll be alone."

"The thralls won't attack without someone to tell them to and the failures are not about to get any closer to the radios. The only time I will be at any risk is while the speakers are off. So get a move on."

I still didn't like the idea, but she was going to be near the car full of weapons, we needed the thralls to evacuate, and the fact that it was completely debilitating to vampires was an unexpected bonus as long as I was out of earshot. I gave her a nod, told her, "Stay safe," and ran down the street. A few blocks away I found a bar in a basement and, ordering a couple fingers of scotch, went to a dark corner table, put the ear plugs back in and sipped my drink, keeping an eye on my watch. I didn't hear anything even eight minutes after I left. Either I was right about the basement helping muffle sound or she hadn't got it back on. I shifted nervously in my seat. What if something had happened and she needed me? I got up and raced up the stairs, but as soon as my head got near street level, the noise began ringing in my head painfully, silenced just enough for me to sheepishly retreat back to my corner.

That was a relief. When the time was supposed to be up, I got up again and this time there was nothing painful about the noise on the street so I unplugged my ears and ran along. This, at least, was something I could enjoy about my new circumstances. I mentioned before that I'd always been a good runner, but now I was passing cars. I jumped over the leash of a dog that was straining against the lady walking it, and must have gone at least five yards horizontally. I made a mental note so I didn't get into a crash overshooting. It was weird, too, because ever since I'd gotten up from the morgue I'd felt kind of stiff and heavy, but once I was really in action, I could move smoothly and easily. It made sense, in a way. I was dead, but I was also a predator by nature, even if I chose not to act that way. Predators have to be either fast and strong, or smart, and at least one category of vampire didn't have brains on their side.

Arriving outside the hotel, it was obvious our plan to get the thralls to evacuate had been generally successful. But without the influence of their masters, their weak physical condition was all the more obvious. Many had just slumped against walls nearby. Others wandered, as if looking for something they couldn't find, and perhaps had forgotten the object of their search. "My God," I whispered. "There must be something we can do to help them."

I called out to Clara. "Is this everyone?"

"I don't know. All the ones able to move on their own, I think, but given the state of them, we'll have to be aware of the possibility of weaker, but still living, people inside."

My heart sank. On some level, I knew these people were victims of the vampires, but only now did it really hit me. Yekaterina was completely complicit in what had happened to others, even if she'd tried to help me. And I blamed myself a little, too, because I was so busy trying to save myself the final day that I didn't think about trying to rescue anyone else. "Irene. Is she here? I was supposed to rescue her and Tammy. They'd killed Tamara already, that's why they said she was gone to a retreat, but Irene was still a thrall when I was captured."

Clara looked around. "I'm not the one who knows her. You find out. I'll get our gear." I went to check on one of the women slumped on the ground. As I approached, a man walked up to me. He was one of the ones who'd been acting as security in the lobby.

"You," I looked him in the eyes. "You're still healthy, aren't you? They'd only take enough from you to get you under their sway."

"You came as a visitor, didn't you?" he asked a bit awkwardly. "What's going on?"

I took a deep breath, calmed myself. He wasn't to blame. Nor was Irene. All of these people were victims. "There's a gas leak in the building. It's made everyone sick, and there could be a fire any minute. I want you to find a phone— don't go back in there, check around the neighborhood. Find a phone and call the hospital. A lot of the people here are pretty damn sick."

He looked around as if noticing everyone for the first time. "I can see that. Yes. They should send ambulances."

I clapped him on the shoulder. "Good man. Get a move on." He started off, leaving me feeling a little relief. As I moved around looking for Irene, I noticed more of the cultists becoming aware of me. Their eyes became more focused. At first I thought that was a good thing, that they were coming back to normal already. Then I worried that they remembered me from when Yekaterina ordered me captured. Neither of those were the case.

As I turned, looking from face to face as they came closer around me, I spotted the woman I'd been looking for. "Hey, Irene." I beckoned to her, "How are you doing?"

"I'm here for you," she said. She was taking off the collar with the funny cross on it.

"What? No, I'm here to help you."

"Yes," said another woman, closer to me. She was also taking off her collar. "Help us feel the holy union again."

"Whoa!" I took a step back and just bumped into two more women behind me. "Oh, no, no, no. I am not that kind of vampire." I jumped up in place and saw Clara ready to go but staring at the small crowd in bemusement. "A little help here!" I called out.

"You don't *need* help," she told me. "You need to show a little authority."

"Right." I calmed myself down mentally and addressed the thralls with my cop voice. "This isn't playtime, people. This building could go at any minute. I need you to move down the street, wait for the ambulances and... if you know your blood type, tell the nice men on the way to the hospital. Go on, all of you." It worked. They left as ordered. I picked up one of the crosses, dropped by a thrall. It didn't bother me, and I still wasn't sure what it meant, so I pocketed it. Glancing up, I saw Clara at the door ready to go and caught up with her. She had one of the shotguns out so I stepped out of the way while I opened the door. Nothing was moving in the lobby that we could see, but I told her, "Let me go through the doors first. I had one drop on me from over a doorway once."

"You take me to the nicest places."

"Should we look for the vampires first or the likely incendiaries?"

"The incendiaries, of course. We don't want to get trapped and burnt, we don't know if there are any other innocents in there, and while I'm deactivating the devices, you can slay anything that attacks."

"I like a woman who knows how to plan."

EXITS

The plan involved me explaining the layout of the place as far as I knew it, and her determining where to search. We went to specific rooms based on where her demolitions and sabotage knowledge said that starting a fire would be most effective. Sure enough, we found the incendiary devices. Wires led from one to another, so we only had to locate one to find the rest. They weren't sophisticated or well-hidden— the two masterminds had no real training in demolitions, and they didn't expect anyone to try to stop their plan. After all, thralls and failures could barely think beyond the moment. Eugene was naively trusting Katie. They had no idea that Clara even existed; I'd made sure not to give a hint. And as for me, well, what were the chances that I'd still care when I woke up? I clearly wasn't normal for a vampire, and putting myself at risk to save people they thought of as food just wouldn't have occurred to them.

Just as Clara had predicted, they'd set charges where the best fuel was. There was one in the kitchen, next to the oven inside a cabinet. When it went, fire would hit the gas pipes and spread out almost instantly to hit all the flammables in the vicinity. Another one was set in the cleaning room, Mop Valhalla: there, the flammable rags, forgotten laundry, and flammable solvents would quickly ignite. The fumes would be nasty, too, and tend to spread quickly because of the dumbwaiters nearby. It occurred to me I should find out if building safety codes had changed since the hotel was built, because it was way too easy to turn the place into a death trap. More wires went to the stairs. All of this was part of the core of the building, not too far apart. But something troubled me. "The lobby area, the courtyard, and the basement. There could be a chance of escape from two of those, and the courtyard has no exit, but it would be relatively safe."

Clara looked over her shoulder at me as she examined the timer connected to the kitchen bomb. "We've got another forty minutes before this needs to be diffused. We should check on the exits. How did you think of those things?"

"You learned how to destroy things for the war.

I learned how to handle evacuations as part of police training. We always need to be aware of exits and safety zones."

We found a couple of small charges above the doors to the lobby. They were set to go off in twenty minutes. "This will be first," I said. "The first area anyone might leave from." Clara didn't simply turn off the timer, as I expected, but took the assembled charges down from the doorframe and removed the detonators from them.

She explained, "This way I make sure there's no backup system to detonate them. And we have something else handy if we need it. Take one."

"For me? And this is only our second date. I didn't get you anything."

In the basement, we saw that it was too late to do anything. The stairs leading to the cellar doors were demolished, ripped apart by hand. And the doors were barred with a crossbeam with the triple-barred cross on it. "Is that a real holy symbol?" I asked Clara.

"Of course!" she said. "It's the Russian Orthodox cross. What did you think it was?"

"Maybe something they just made up?"

"I noticed people wearing them when we got the building evacuated. It would keep the thralls from being eaten by the lesser vampires."

Speaking of lesser vampires. It occurred to me that going underground to dampen the sonic weapon had worked for me, and might work for others. "Clara, start back up the stairs," I suggested. She only took one step before Vagrant rushed out from behind the barrels toward her. I pivoted. She slowly, it seemed to me, raised the shotgun to shoulder height, but the monster was getting closer by the millisecond. I leaped to intercept him, tackling him and pulling him to the side. As we tumbled, I heard the shotgun blast, loud and deep and yards away. Vagrant and I were on a different scale of time and distance from the mortal world, as we fought. He was hungry for Clara's blood, but I was furious at him for it and getting in two or more hits for any he managed. Like before, when I ran, fighting was making me feel more alive, more real, more awake.

Because I was acting on instinct, I hadn't drawn a weapon right away. Clara couldn't use her shotgun again because the only way to hit either of us would pepper us both. I've never been peppered with salt, but I'm glad she held back. Meanwhile, I gouged open Vagrant's cheek with my nails on one of my punches, and the blood welling out, thick and dark, smelled sour and bitter but also tempting. He howled, not with pain, but rage and need as he fought back and ended up biting me on the shoulder. I shoved him back, ignoring the tearing of my own flesh, and took the wooden musket ball with the prayer for the dead written on it and shoved it in his mouth. I thought I smelled something smokey, but I didn't wait for the result before pulling out my homemade stake and shoving it into his chest.

I let go of him then and waited, watching his aura. It was the first one I'd seen that was all black, and it broke apart and dropped away from him. When it was gone, his face was peaceful. I checked him over quickly for ID or dog tags. The tags— WWI— were around his neck and I took them. I'd try and locate his family later and notify them of his death. He'd gone down fighting Rasputin, and he must have had some strength in him still, because he was the oldest of this batch of failed vampires, but he'd not rotted like the rest of them. There had been enough of a brain left for him to take cover, too. I felt oddly sad, too aware we each could have been in the other's position.

"Rafael?" Clara's voice broke into my thoughts. "Mmm?"

"You're licking your fingers."

I looked at my hands. There were a few traces left of the blood I'd drawn during the fight. I had licked the rest clean without thinking. I rubbed the remainder off on the coat I was wearing, embarrassed. "Let's see what they did to the courtyard. I thought it wasn't an exit, but I hadn't thought about flying."

The way up had been cut off there, too. "Vampires have some power over animals, and are particularly known to use vermin," Clara said. A ceiling had been created over the courtyard by layers and layers of spiderwebs. "They must have summoned acres worth of spiders to do it, though."

"Rasputin's powerful," I said. "And I'm not just talking about his smell. Although getting dumped in the river by his would-be assassins is definitely the last time he took a bath."

Clara surveyed the rest of the yard, covered with debris. "It looks like they figure the webs and rubbish will burn this area as well. Let's go back and I'll disarm the main timer."

I held the guns while she worked on the device. I'd just as soon not get into close combat again right now. I didn't like how savagely I'd fought or my taste for blood after. I was glad of my choice when I saw Cataracts crawling toward us along the ceiling. Cataracts had blood dripping from her ears, an after-effect of the long exposure to the sonic dispersal device, and I'm not sure what had led her to us with her vision and hearing presumably impaired. Maybe scent.

Her aura was all black, like Vagrant's— actually John Hardy from his dog tags— had been. It was obviously the color of the vampire itself. I shot her with the salt cartridge. People do that sometimes on human trespassers, but it definitely had more of an effect on a vampire. She screamed and dropped to the ground. She flipped herself upright, looked like she was going to charge, but flopped to her stomach and, while her body spasmed, began reaching her arms toward us. They were stretching a monstrous length, and had come halfway to us by the time I had the handgun lined up for my shot. The wooden bullet went through the open space of the shoulder girdle and into her heart. Her mouth stopped screeching and let out a torrent of dark liquid. The black aura of the vampire left her at the same time. Once it did, her arms shrunk back to normal length. I didn't bother searching her for ID. She wore the cult robes, which didn't have pockets. Besides, there should be one more failure around, Gangrene, and I wasn't going to leave watching over Clara.

"Done," she told me, "In spite of the racket." She looked over at the body. "You had to deal with these things alone before."

"Yeah. It was pretty harrowing." If Yekaterina hadn't been keeping a close eye on things, I probably would have been eaten by them before Rasputin ever saw me. "I didn't know what they were are the time, though. And they didn't act quite like that. Still, you could tell there was something wrong. There's just one left, unless they created more, and I don't think they did that often. Yekaterina was surprised Rasputin wanted to turn me. After we find the last one, we should make sure the building is clear, and then..."

"Then?"

"I think maybe you should reconnect the timer. We can't explain this. I hate to say it, but the Russians were right about not leaving evidence." It went against my instincts for fairness, truth, and preservation, but there was no way that shooting a rotting carcass in self-defense would make sense in a court of law. Not to mention, I was a dead man myself, and being investigated would not be in my best interests.

"Now you're thinking like covert ops."

"But I'm worried about the neighborhood."

"I'll make it so only one goes off. The fire will spread slower, still take care of the evidence, but firefighters will be able to keep it contained."

Well, I'd knocked out an innocent man, stolen

an overcoat, and discharged firearms within city limits. Looked like accessory to arson would be added onto St. Peter's list of charges, should I ever be called to proper account. "That will have to do."

We started a room to room search, but with six stories to worry about, and the need to rescue Eugene and stop the ringleaders, the pressure was on. As we walked, opening doors, I tried to think of a way to save time. "You said vampires can control animals?"

"Yes. What are you thinking?"

THE DINING ROOM

"There are a lot of rats in this neighborhood."

"I could have gone my whole life without knowing that," she responded drily.

"They're going to comb the building for us." I concentrated. I closed my eyes and thought about rats. It felt like I opened my eyes again, but no, not mine, I was seeing a jumbled kaleidoscope of images, mostly dark. I heard a crowd of voices, the sound of cars, a vacuum, tinny music, a yowling cat that made my hairs stand on end, hungry children squeaking. Apparently, I wasn't just able to summon and command them. I could be them.

I pulled myself back into me for a moment. "You be the lookout, Clara," I said. "I'm going to be elsewhere for a while."

"Where are you going?" she asked.

"Everywhere," I told her. And then I went. Some of us were already in the building. The rest, the others, every rat I could feel in a four block radius, and that was a lot, I impelled to come to the hotel, and then left only a thread of myself with them while they moved. The ones here, I rode with, feeling boards and concrete beneath our tiny paws, smelling, listening, peeking for signs of life. Sometimes, running through a tight area tickled our whiskers. I kind of liked that feeling.

The basement had nothing but the body. I pulled one of the exploring rats off it before we could take a bite. Okay, this power was kind of cool, but definitely had a gross side. The first floor was almost empty. "There's a woman in the ceremonial room." I said it out loud, because I felt Clara touch my shoulder, mine, not the shoulder of any of the furry little bodies I was also in, and it helped be reorganize my thoughts back in my head. "She was breathing. Let's get her out."

We did so, and by the time I'd carried her out to the sidewalk, we could see there were already attendants busy helping people into ambulances. I took her over. "Hey, this one's in worse shape than the others. Get her to the emergency room."

"What's going on here?" the ambulance worker demanded.

"These guys were in a cult. Low blood count. I think the leaders may have made them do some kind of ritual bloodletting to keep them weak, confused and docile. I used to be a cop, and was running a private investigation on them. Get her to the hospital, and come back."

I ran back in while he got on his radio. There would be more emergency services soon, so we needed to finish up fast. With that in mind, I locked the door behind me, sat at Clara's feet, and went back into the rats. They'd found out more. Only the second and third floors showed signs of recent occupancy— the upper floors, the resident rats' memory told me, held only old fabric and wood to interest them. And toilet bowls to drink out of. Sharing a mind with an animal definitely had its down side.

But the second floor had a room with multiple beds. It had been built as a private dining room when the hotel expected prosperous guests and special occasion rentals, making its current use eerily appropriate. The people here hadn't gotten up when the sound started to irritate them because they, like the woman in the orgy room, were too weak to walk. The vampires had taken too much and they were waiting to recover... or not.

But the sound had also injured the already damaged Gangrene, and he, like Rasputin, was driven to heal by feeding. He knew where the food was gathered. The rats had seen the dried blood crusted under his ears. His teeth glistened with saliva as he bent down over another bed. "STOP HIM!" I shouted.

That was out loud, too, obviously. This time, Clara was pulling me to my feet. "Where?!" she demanded.

"Second floor. Dining room. Wing near the freight elevator." She tugged on my hand to start me running with her while I tried to remember how long my legs were and how many I had. I think a part of me was still with the rats, as I heard Gangrene howl and thought I could scent the faint aroma of vampire blood.

"The rats are going to be there when we get there," I mentioned.

"I'm not scared of them, Raf," she said, "I'm just not enamored."

"They're also going to be busy," I pointed out.

"Just with the vampire, right?"

"Right."

"I'm fine with that."

"Let's use the holy water," I suggested. "I'm starting to like my little vermin friends. They don't need to catch friendly fire. One's a mother."

"You continue to be sentimental in the most surprising ways."

We were almost there. The animal noises coming from the rats and from Gangrene were clearly audible to Clara, too, now. I guess he couldn't control them, or at least, couldn't wrench them away from my control once I'd started with them. Whatever his exact limitations were, the little rodents were keeping him distracted from further feedings. Clara loaded the shotgun with fresh shells outside the door, then nodded to me. I opened the door while she held the weapon ready.

It wasn't a pretty sight. Gangrene was covered in tiny wounds, while, sadly, the floor was littered with the bodies of fallen rats. Well, it was surprising that I was sentimental about them, except I'd been inside their little minds and knew them. There were still more fighting him, and more arriving to replace the fallen.

Clara stepped forward through the doorway and fired. The first shot rang out and the rats scattered in alarm at the sound. The shell broke open, spraying out a small amount of holy water in a misty cone that turned into rainbows as it crossed in front of a chandelier. It hit Gangrene and his skin began to melt, blistering and sizzling. He tried to take mist form himself, but that didn't help when she fired the second shell and mist of holy water met the unholy mist form of the vampire.

The black aura of vampirism was completely vaporized. In this case, so were the remains. Everything just vanished. The room had no more vampire, only some rather confused rodents who I quickly released to leave the building. The beds in the dining room/infirmary held bodies, for the most part. I didn't have to pause to take pulses; either there was an aura, and with it, life, or there wasn't. Gangrene had been gorging himself, I thought, probably in part to make up for how little food his masters had allowed him before. There were only two left to save. One was one of the elderly followers. She wasn't too pale; I thought it likely she had some other condition that had been exacerbated by the strain of being made a thrall. The other one was a young Asian woman, maybe just a girl. I picked up the two survivors, one with each arm.

"I'll get them out. Once we know that no one else has come in, you can re-rig the incendiaries. It should be safe now. "

I did encounter some policemen gathering outside, waiting to go in. There were fewer ambulances now. The ones that were there were apparently on their second round of pick ups, as they rather smoothly handled intake on the remaining thralls. I turned over the ones I had rescued to the lead officer, who put some of his men in charge of getting stretchers for them. Meanwhile, I explained that my partner had found some kind of explosive device and was trying to dismantle it. "No one else has gone in yet, have they?"

"No. But get him out, we'll get the bomb squad."

"Her, actually. Radio it in. I'll let her know to come out. The rest of the building is empty, so it can wait." I'd only gotten as far as the back of the lobby when Clara came hurrying along. I gave her a wink to let her know everything was okay.

She shouted, "There was a secondary detonator. Clear the area!"

I double-timed it out of there with her. No running. We already knew we had time and that the blast would be limited. Mostly, I didn't want to risk running too fast in front of an audience, since I was still learning control. Why Clara didn't, well, I supposed she needed to act less urgent at first, until she was assured the building was clear, and it wouldn't make sense to run at the end.

The officer in charge wanted a statement from me as we cleared the stairs in front, but I shook my head and gave him my business card. "Look me up later for the explanation," I told him. "I have to stop my client from making a terrible mistake." He only hesitated a moment before giving me a nod. They still had issues to deal with now, it was late at night, there was time for paperwork later.

As we got into the car and closed the doors, there was a deep noise, *whump*, like a muffled but amplified version of the sound a gas stove makes when it catches alight. Clara and I exchanged glances and then had to stifle a laugh. It might not be the appropriate response to committing arson, but we'd done something audacious and gotten away with it. Not just the arson: the whole scheme, vampire hunting, had been dangerous, but also almost surreal. We were laughing with relief as much as anything. "You were brilliant," I said. "You're amazing."

"You weren't so bad yourself, hot shot." She gave me a smile.

"I love that you've got a sense of adventure like I do. I want us to be like this forever." I'd been leaning forward ready to kiss her, when it struck me. Forever. What I was now wasn't who I was a few days ago. I was going to be this way forever. And this wasn't going to work. I had too much power and too many of the wrong instincts now. I was sickened at the thought of ever making someone like me, much less the risk of creating a failure, but the alternative seemed pretty bleak, too.

I turned, instead to face forward and start the car. "But forever's too long," I concluded.

She looked at me, a little disappointed, but mostly appraising my reaction. I guess she had an idea of where my mind was, and figured the best way to stop me ruminating was to get me back in action. "We need to get to whatever the main international port is. I think they're more likely to travel by ship than by plane."

"Why?"

"More control over how much light they get. If a plane doesn't run to schedule, it could be very hard for them to avoid daylight, and they'd be above the clouds. In a ship, they only have to worry about a shipwreck and they could be sure of getting a lifeboat."

"That makes sense. I can't believe I'm going to have to be worrying about things like that."

"Will you have to sleep by day?"

"I haven't been this way for more than a few hours, but I don't think so. I think it's more of a convenience thing, since they can't go out in the sun. That is, I saw Yekaterina during the day at Eugene's. She was having him work on a fire suppressant. Now that I know it's one of their vulnerabilities, her weirdness then makes more sense." I took a left turn. "The Brooklyn Port Authority. It's close, it's busy, they're likely to choose it for handiness, and if they didn't, as long as the people in charge there will listen to you, they can contact the other ports and airports and even the train stations. New York was built on solid rock... and on being one of the best paths for moving products and people."

BE A BAT

Arriving at the harbor, I looked at the row of ships in dismay. The number that were large enough for a transatlantic voyage were at least a few dozen, and each of them probably had as much space as the hotel we'd just left. There were a lot of big buildings for processing travelers and cargo, too. We needed a clear idea of where to begin and even with that, we'd have to search intelligently and know the timetable.

Clara went to talk to the port authorities, but I thought I'd take a look around on my own. If the vampires had already gotten on board a ship, I wanted to be sure they couldn't launch before I caught up with them. I'm generally not a vengeful man, but being hunted and eaten is hard not to take personally. There might not be enough blood in my veins, but I had plenty of anger flowing. So I decided to try to use my new powers to get an aerial view.

First, I needed to turn into a bat. I assumed I could do that; so far, most of the legends were true if you took into account that the difference between failure and elite vampires weren't something people were aware of. I closed my eyes and tried exerting my will. "Be a bat, be a bat," I repeated in a low voice, hoping no one passed by too closely to me in the parking lot and overheard. It became clear that this was not how shape-shifting worked. I didn't know; there wasn't a manual on how to be a vampire.

I tried to relax and use my imagination. I'd seen bats up close sometimes. In particular, back in Europe, there was a squad of Royal Australian Air Force pilots who kept a bat as their mascot. He was big, and had a face that was canine-like enough you could understand why it was called a flying fox. I imagined shrinking, face melting back until I had the pointy snout, fingers stretching, prickly little talons on my feet. I could see the bat in my mind's eye and when I opened my real eyes, I found they were only a few feet above the ground. I held up a foot. Oh, yes, there was the fur and claws. I wondered briefly where my clothes were. Apparently the magic extended to them, which was good. I flapped my wings a couple of times, or tried to. I jumped and flapped again. I lost my balance, fell on my side, and righted myself. Maybe, I thought, I just needed to take off from altitude. There were some large birds that did that, right? Awful on the ground, but graceful in the air.

I tried climbing a lamppost nearby. That wasn't hard at all; my claws easily found gripping points, and I made it to the top. Hanging upside down, I spread my wings and released my grip. I can at least say I slowed my descent, but what I managed was more a sort of tumble through the air than a flight and I picked my dignity and my butt off the ground near the edge of the parking lot, scrambled into a shadowed area, and changed back into my normal form.

With a few seconds more thought, I focused on what my teeth ought to feel like and gave myself a fang-free smile in the side mirror of the nearest car. Nice to know I could pass for human, but then I thought about how easily other monsters could. Just then, a whistle blew, and one of the ocean liners began to slowly pull away from the dock, ready to head out to sea. Chances were, that wasn't the one we were after; the name and flags suggested a Caribbean cruise, and fun in the sun was pretty much the opposite of what vampires wanted. Nevertheless, it was a reminder that time wasn't in our favor.

Then I saw Clara heading back my way, which put me in a happier frame of mine. She must have found out Eugene's location, so I ran to join her.

"He's here. We shouldn't have much trouble getting him, I think, but the vampires are a problem. The plan worked— they pretended there was some kind of problem with his passport while virtually ignoring the other two. They went on ahead to get the cabins ready without him. They're probably suspicious."

"We get him clear first. We don't want them to come back for him. If they really are suspicious, they're probably paving the way to take him without official approval. He's got to be out of the area and under guard."

"I know that, Raf. I knew about vampires before you did, remember?"

"Sorry." I gave her a smile.

"Say, what happened to the fangs?"

"I started experimenting with shape-shifting."

"Useful for long term, but it seems like you might have wanted something more relevant to the situation."

"I was actually trying to turn into a bat for aerial reconnaissance."

"That's sensible. But you couldn't do it?"

"I could transform. But I couldn't fly."

She looked surprised. "We'll work on that. But why didn't you use control over animals again?"

"There's plenty of rats around, but I wanted a view from the air."

She lifted her head to look at the roof of the building we were heading for. I followed her gaze. There were about ten gulls on the near edge alone. There were more on the posts of the docks, and then there were the ones flapping from ship to ship. "Can I do that? They were never mentioned in *Dracula*."

"People do consider them pests."

"Huh. Sea gulls. Pigeons. There's some very practical sleuthing potential through control of animals." We were inside the building now and let discussion of my powers drop in the name of discretion.

NOT YOUR GIRLFRIEND

Eugene was being kept in a waiting area with a couple with a small child, and many empty chairs. He looked up at us in surprise. "Rafael! I'm so glad you're here. The most ridiculous mix-up has happened. They said someone already left the country with my passport, and they can't release me to go to France with my fiancee until they check on his identity and clear things up. I showed them my driver's license and they've phoned the police to verify it, but if you will just vouch for me, I'm sure we can get this all straightened out much faster."

I nodded to the uniform behind the reception desk. Clara did more than that, going over with something in writing that I assumed authorized his release to us. "Let me see your ticket." He handed it over and I examined it, getting the name of the ship and the dock and berth information. "It's going to be okay, Eugene. But not because you're leaving with your fiancee. We asked them to detain you for your own safety. Those two aren't who you think they are and just wanted you to gain a tactical advantage."

"Don't be ridiculous. Katie loves me. Why else would she ask me to marry her and go to France for our honeymoon? Why would she bring her father along?"

I tried not to roll my eyes. "That woman is not your girlfriend, Eugene," I said.

He blinked in confusion. "Are you sure? I really thought it was her."

I realized he had misunderstood me. With his difficulty with faces, he thought I meant he was eloping with the wrong girl. I hated to trick him, but it was suddenly obvious that it would be easier to get him to safety building on that, rather than trying to convince him that his Katie was just using him. "I'm sure, Eugene. That lady does look rather similar, but her name is Yekaterina. She's a Russian. I'm afraid she's just been using your girlfriend's name. She's been imitating Katie's voice, too. Her real voice has quite a thick accent." All of which was true.

"She had me completely fooled!" That was true, too.

"Yekaterina's part of a criminal gang that

specializes in exploiting people. Now, I'm going to make sure that she and her partner get what's coming to them, but I think you should go home with Clara now for your safety. Her partner is a very dangerous man."

Clara looked at me. "He *is* very dangerous."

I gave my head a little shake. "The only thing I have left to lose is the people I care about. I want you both out of here."

Clara didn't like that, I could tell, but she didn't argue. She just said, "I expect you to catch up with us before morning," and passed the handgun along to me. She put her hand on Eugene's arm and began to lead him away.

He turned to look back at me over his shoulder. "I want you to stop them and find the real Katie for me!"

"Just go, Eugene," I said. "I'll explain more later." That was going to be awkward. He wasn't good with dishonesty, which was why he hired me and some highly skilled and loyal lawyers to protect him from bad faith dealing by others. I had to hope that I wouldn't lose his trust once he understood the full situation. Meanwhile, I made time to *La Belle Océan Bleu,* the ship specified on his ticket.

"KILL HIM"

I went up the gangplank with several other people, but found myself hesitating strangely just before I could step onto the deck. It didn't feel right, like I was thinking of crossing crime scene tape without permission. Or as if there was a curtain I had to push through. I had only paused for a couple of seconds when I was greeted by the purser. "Sir, you can give your ticket here." I gratefully stepped onto the deck and showed him Eugene's ticket. "Hello, Mr. Marshall. Your friends are waiting for you."

"I'm sure they are," I said. "Any idea where?"

"They're on the bridge with the captain. Father Putin expressed an interest in seeing the radio and navigation equipment."

"Really? He never struck me as very technically minded."

The officer shrugged. "Often people just like to feel important enough to be given a tour. The captain tries to be accommodating. So many people are going to the airplanes now. We're having to take cargo as well, you know, to make the voyage pay."

"Hard times," I said sympathetically. "I think I should see them before going to the cabin."

"That's fine. Go to the upper deck, and it will be the first room on the prow end."

I nodded and found the stairs. I was a little over halfway up when the purser caught up with me. "Perhaps you should wait," he said. "There may be some problem. The captain wants to see me."

"Oh, yeah, I think there's a problem." I stopped and turned, blocking the stairway. The vampires had tried giving me orders. For some reason, I hadn't cared too much, other than to feel a kind of pressure from their stare, but it was worth trying it myself now. "But the captain does *not* want you up there. He wants you to stop further boarding until you are told otherwise, and all passengers already boarded should go to their cabins and stay there." I fixed his eyes with mine and tried to impress my words into his brain as if they were the most important thing he would ever hear.

"Yessir," he responded, as if I was the captain and had every right to give such a command. He turned and headed back down. That should limit the ability of the vampires to take hostages or cause collateral damage. I headed the rest of the way to the bridge at a run, a real run, taking the stairs three at a time. Rasputin and Yekaterina were up to mischief with the officers, that was certain.

With large windows on the sides, I could see into the bridge as I approached the door. I saw the two lead vampires for the first time since my death.

Seeing Rasputin now awoke a new sense of horror. The failed vampires had had auras made entirely of the black goo, but small, extending only inches beyond their decaying bodies. Rasputin, however, was orbited by the stuff. It extended for yards all around him, briefly touching and clinging to people nearby. Some part of it even seemed to be sticking to their auras. That, I suspected, was connected to his ability to sway people's minds, placing them under his control. In fact, it looked like he'd gathered most of the officers on the ship and placed them under his sway. As long as they were taking orders from him, the Port Authority couldn't stop Katie or Rasputin from going back to Eugene and taking him on board.

Speaking of Katie, Yekaterina had the black stuff that meant vampirism woven around an aura of gray flame. It seemed to me to be more extensive than mine, but like me, she had some moments of color, vibrant flares as her passionate nature was aroused. It was flickering with a deep rose now as she wrapped her arms around the first mate. I winced as she bit into his neck, then a sense of moral outrage took over. She was as evil as Rasputin— not as crazy, but maybe worse because I believed that like me, she had a choice about her actions. She chose to be selfish, to take what she wanted and make others suffer so she could feel better for a while. I couldn't allow that. Not for myself to do it and certainly not to stand and watch another vampire attack.

I rushed into the room. "Let him go!" I ordered.

I was a little surprised that Yekaterina actually released the first mate, stepping away from him. "Kill him," she said.

The first mate drew a pistol and fired at me. I twisted and the bullet only grazed my shoulder.

Yekaterina shouted. "Are you both stupid!?" She looked at me. "I meant *you* should kill," she indicated the first mate with a tilt of her head, "*him*." She continued looking at me in disbelief. "You look so hungry."

Now it was my turn to be shocked. "I'm not like you! I came to stop the pair of you."

Rasputin caught on faster than she did, unsurprisingly. "Stop *this*," he sneered, using extended nails to slice a gash across the Captain's neck and pushing him at me. I ran forward and caught the man before he could fall on his face, but the smell of blood so close, so fresh, made me salivate. I needed to stop the bleeding, but how could I trust myself?

Rasputin elbowed out the window and jumped out, down to one of the lower decks. Yekaterina hesitated. "I thought you were going to help me."

"*This* is who needs help," I growled, holding the Captain. None of the rest of the crew were moving. I looked up at them and saw that the black ooze aura of Rasputin was still clinging to them. That made me angry, not at them, but for them. How dare he deaden their natural responses. How dare he leave this man to bleed, as if none of them mattered, as if life didn't matter. "*Help him!*" I gave the order in frustration, but when I did it, my own aura lashed out, not the black, contaminated bits, but bright vermilion flames of light that burned the blackness away. With nothing more strange than a tiny red spark embedded in their own auras, the men awoke to the world around them and snapped into action. Two of them took the Captain from my arms. One placed a handkerchief to the wound, which now that I saw it from a distance, hadn't bled as much as I thought. A third man lunged for a leather bag. He had to be the ship's doctor. Good, they'd be all right.

Yekaterina still wasn't gone. I pulled out the pistol, but she was already moving. Moving close to me, not running away. "Oh, soldier boy," she said, "I know what you're doing. I tried to resist it, too, at first. As if we could make ourselves human again by refusing to feed."

"I have fed," I growled. I should have shot her, I guess, but it was hard to override my reluctance to kill. She seemed so human compared to the others. "Not on the living. You could have done the same."

She paused. "Perhaps it's not enough. You don't seem sated."

I wasn't. I wanted to lick the fresh blood off my hands. I stared at them. I wanted to bite her. I suspected she might be messing with my head, but her aura was keeping to herself. "It *has* to be enough."

She thought a moment. "It took a lot of force to free them from Rasputin." My eyes flicked back up to meet hers. "The more we use our powers, the more we burn through our supply."

I groaned and thought about how I'd wasted mine. "I should never have tried being a bat."

She reached out and stroked my hair. "If you're going to take down Rasputin, you're going to need to know what you're doing. You need a teacher."

I pushed away from her. "You need a slayer. Unless you're willing to go on the wagon." I leveled the gun at her head. "Say what I need to hear. Tell me you'll stop hurting people." I really didn't want to have to shoot her. She was the only vampire so far that was anything like me, and if she really couldn't help but prey on people, maybe there was no hope for me to keep my sanity and values intact. "I'll help you get on the straight and narrow, Princess, but I need you to say you'll try."

"We'll talk again later, guardsman" was all she had to say, as she began to disperse as a mist. I fired, but the load was wooden bullets and with two sent through her vapor form without result, it was clear I'd waited too long.

"Are you mad, American, or are we?" The officers were looking at me now, except for the doctor, still occupied with the captain, and the first mate who was gazing vaguely in the direction Yekaterina had left in.

"No one's sane tonight," I told him. I tapped open a conspicuous cabinet and found what I was hoping to, in the form of a bottle. "I need this booze more than the captain does right now, and I'm sure there's a bar somewhere on the ship when you're ready to unwind." I re-holstered the pistol as a sign of good faith. "The simple version of what's going on is: I'm here to help. You do not want the long version."

I left then, no powers, just heading out the door and scouting the ship visually. Giving it more thought, I went ahead and used my power to control animals to have the gulls scout the open part of the ship. If nothing else, it helped me eliminate places and narrow down the possibilities. As I strode along, I snatched birds out of the air and drank. They gave me far more energy than I spent on controlling them. I felt guilty and embarrassed to do it. It's not like I was a vegetarian, but consuming something that used to be living is something one comes to terms with. This was different, in part because I could see their aura, the soft flicker of life energy around them that went gray and then disappeared as I took their blood and their life force. The experience was different than drinking bottled blood. My own aura seemed to be growing stronger in the process.

Another thing that made biting the gulls different from eating chicken was I had to put my mouth right on their feathers, and these birds had been through dirty water and smoke. Some of them frankly made me want to gag until the blood started flowing and washed the nastiness away. Fastidiousness wasn't an option tonight, I felt. If blood was power and I needed it to fight Rasputin, I had to take care of it before I reached a point where I might lose control.

Weapons would also be better than powers. The handgun was fine if the vampires were solid, but I needed to have a plan for if they weren't.

I started to walk past a gift shop but saw something in the window that gave me an idea. I said to the clerk, "That display of perfume atomizers? I need them."

"Very good, sir. What's your cabin number?"

I tutted. "I don't want them delivered. I want to take them with me when I walk out of here."

"I mean for the billing."

Oh, this was good. I wouldn't have to pull any magic influence to get them. "Cabin B15. Eugene Marshall." We should all live like the swells.

He wrote that down. "Do you need these gift wrapped?"

"Just enough paper so they don't break in the bag," I told him.

"And we have a fine selection of perfumes over

there." He indicated a glass case further in with his pen.

"No, thanks. I already know what I want to fill these with." Holy water. It did the job even when a vampire was in mist form, provided the water was aerosolized, too. In fact, it worked better that way, able to reach every molecule of them. And a ship this fancy would certainly have a chapel. Even though they would probably have more than one type of service, there must be communion wafers, holy water, etc, even if they had to swap out what ones they used between services.

HIDE AND SEEK

Once I had my bag of atomizers, I went in search of the chapel. One of the gulls that was still circling the ship saw a cross on a door near the middle starboard side of the main deck. I went for it. The cross was plain, not a crucifix, but a good, all purpose symbol for Christians. I touched it for a moment. My hand didn't hurt. If anything, I felt soothed by the sight. Reaching lower, I turned the handle and let myself in.

Something smashed into my back. I dropped the bag and gasped for breath as a crushing grip went around my neck. The smell hit me. "Little brother," Rasputin's deep voice rumbled in my ear, "how nice of you to play hide and seek with me."

I threw an elbow back into him, aiming low to try to get under the ribcage. Vampires aren't immune to pain and a bruised liver might hurt enough to get him off me. A grunt and a groaning wheezing exhalation showed me I'd hurt him, but the shortness of the sound meant he was used to rough and tumble. I'd use the gun, but I couldn't reach it because of the hold he had me in. I thought I might try pure strength— for all that he was bigger than me, we still weighed the same as normal people, so if I jumped backwards, I could slam us against the wall with him playing the shoe between my hammer and the wall's anvil.

He had his own idea about how it should go. He was forcing me over to the font, and once I realized that, I went along with only a token struggle as he ranted. "It's good you sought us out. But no nonsense about stopping us. You should be working with us. You are stronger now, but once you understand who has the real strength, you will comply." He started to force my hand down into the holy water. Suddenly, I plunged in to halfway up my forearm, taking his hand along for the ride.

He bellowed as the skin melted and sizzled. By the time he lifted his hand out of the water, raw muscle and tendon was shown, and tatters of skin, still smoking, hung from his wrist. He had released me this time. The fanatic gleam showed in his eyes. "The lord Christ lets us share his suffering," he interpreted his pain with a genuflection to a cross on the wall.

"He didn't boil during his baptism," I reminded

him. I had tucked my hand under my coat quickly, as if trying to hide the injury, but really, I was grabbing the pistol and releasing the safety. I was twisted to one side, too, allowing me to take aim with the weapon parallel to my chest. I fired, ruining the coat, but giving him no forewarning. It was good, going into the center of his chest. Unfortunately, the second shot went into his shoulder as the impact and pain moved him.

I'd love to report that was it for him. But the load had been too strong on the round that hit his chest. It had gone straight through and lodged in the wall behind him. That's the trouble with experimental weaponry. Being in such close quarters hadn't helped, either. Vampire hunting should be done from a distance, if you're a human and want to survive. In my case, what I cared about was effectiveness.

Close quarters with a gun and a bullet-resistant foe isn't really good, period. He punched me hard enough in the face I heard bone crack. My vision got really wobbly and there was no way to aim. I didn't want to waste bullets so I swung the gun like a small club, hoping to clock him or at least discourage him from following up. It worked, I guess, because the dark blur in front of me moved, and disappeared.

I groped back to the font and splashed some of the water on my face. It helped and I began to feel my head clear. This wasn't going well. I had expected it to be pretty much a fight between equals now. After all, I was a vampire, too. I had the same powers. But having your hands on a set of keys doesn't make you a driver. They'd had years of using their powers, whether to protect themselves or attack. I'd had a matter of hours, most of which time I'd spent trying to act as human as possible.

I started to fill the atomizers. They were still my best weapon to use on the mist forms and I figured I'd need to use the tools I knew while I was figuring out how to fight better with my new skills. It helped that I'd managed to give Rasputin some grief even before being turned. Fitting dance steps into my fighting moves had left him confused: he was all brutal force, no finesse.

A scream broke through my musings. I just had two atomizers ready, but it could be enough. I tucked them into my pockets and ran towards the sound. I doubted Rasputin had retraced my steps, it was just that the sales clerk was nearby and in an easily spotted situation. The mad monk needed to heal himself and he was at the clerk's throat.

"No more deaths!" I shouted and sprayed some

of the holy water on the pair of them. Rasputin couldn't ignore the threat and dropped his victim. Fortunately, the wound seemed to be closing unnaturally fast and I could see the clerk was breathing.

"Little brother, you're being absurd. Everyone dies. I died, you died. The difference between us and most is that, like Christ, we arose on the third day."

I executed a jump kick that hit him on the chin and knocked him into a display at the back of the little shop. One of the strange things about the vampire form was that it wasn't more durable, but it healed better, and in spite of being much stronger, didn't have any more mass, so now that I was on his level I understood how he could have pitched me across several lanes of traffic so easy.

I didn't hesitate to follow up, either. The idea was to force him to keep reacting to me instead of letting him plan, attack, and heal between bouts anymore. That was good as an idea, but I found out quickly enough how hard it was to execute. Thankfully, since he knew I'd put together a holy water spritz for him, he kept himself tangible. Even being able to reach him, I had to deal with the fact he was a lot taller than me and while he was lean framed, it was all muscle. At least I knew how to use my whole body in a fight and he had a devil of a time keeping up with me with speed and moves developed on a dance floor. I managed to flip him over my back after dodging a lunge from him and threw him through the window and out onto the main deck.

As the fight continued, I was finding myself becoming more limber, and even starting to sweat a little. All the muscle movements were raising my body temperature to the level of the living. I started to get optimistic again. He wasn't going to stay put, but I might be able to wear him down until he slowed enough for me to try another heart shot, or with a little luck, the ship might have an axe or machete near the lifeboats for speed in cutting the ropes.

Then he turned into a wolf and sank teeth into my shoulder. I lost one of the holy water atomizers as he knocked me for a loop. He released the shoulder, I think intending to go for the throat, but I kept going with the somersault and then turned it into a sideways roll, slamming him into a wall. I heard him whine as I got to my feet but as I spun to face him, I found he'd turned half into mist, leaving his hands free to pummel me. I smiled, ready to reach for the last holy water atomizer, when I found out the hard way he also had a solid knee.

The crotch is just as much vulnerable on a male vampire as it is on the living, believe me. For a moment I was lost in a fog of pain. I heard his voice again. "I'll leave you to think it over, little brother. If you insist on opposing me, you will never have anything but pain. But if you are willing to accept what you are now, Yekaterina and I can show you what power and pleasures it can bring."

I heard him walking away. There were still tears in my eyes but I straightened up and pulled the gun. I fired again. It passed through him. The monster had left the center of his torso misted. One bullet left. I swore and tucked the gun back out of the way. Running after him, I pulled out the atomizer. Just before I could get close enough to spray him, he turned and swung a fist. "You're lucky I'm letting you have this tantrum," he said as the blow sent me flying sideways. "Change is difficult. Katya wouldn't eat for three days."

She hadn't been lying about trying to resist it at first. Did that mean she could give up being a killer now, or did it mean I wouldn't be able to keep my human values in the long term? It was a fair question, I thought, as I pulled myself to my feet. Even without using powers myself, all this fast healing was taking its toll on me. It didn't help to hear more shots, look up, and find some of the officers were firing onto the deck. They didn't have the right kind of load. They couldn't kill me or him. But from where I saw splinters flying, I didn't think they were being choosy about their aim. At least one of them hadn't trusted me, and the thought flashed through my mind that if they couldn't trust me, maybe they shouldn't. Would one person's blood for the strength to stop Rasputin be a fair trade? "God, no," I answered myself out loud. It wasn't really me thinking that, it was the dark stuff, the vampire blood Rasputin had contaminated me with. I looked back at him.

"And you?"

"I fed on a Cossack an hour after I rose. It was fantastic! The first day of the rest of my life." He grinned. I grabbed the pistol again, hoping he was too busy gloating to think about using his mist form. I realized then the other gunfire had stopped and looked up. The officers were under control again. This time, Yekaterina had put them in a trance.

"You forgot something!" Yekaterina yelled, throwing something metal that flashed when it caught the light as it tumbled through the air. I reached up for it reflexively, and it punctured my hand, in the bit of flesh between fingers. It was the lock pick that I'd left in her. Her trying to puncture my head with it was understandable, I guess, but it wouldn't have gone through bone as easily as soft tissue and she hadn't thrown it that well. Or had she thrown it to me, not at me? Now I had a weapon in hand that had already proven itself good enough to reach the heart and paralyze an elite vampire.

While I'd been distracted, Rasputin had decided to take the offensive. I turned back to him to see the wolf form leaping at me. I started to dodge right but he caught me on the left arm, teeth sinking in. As his momentum pulled me down again, I curled in toward him, bringing in the lock pick and stabbing it into his chest. It was a damn shame he was in wolf form, because the chest was a different shape, his heart wasn't placed right for what I'd tried. His eyes swiveled to look at me. If he'd been a real beast I'd think he was rabid. We hit the ground and the pistol dropped out of my left hand.

Well, the form he had taken had great teeth but no hands and I had one free to punch with. With the wolf straddling me, I gave it my best and it turned out, wolves have plenty sensitive family jewels, too. His jaws gaped open in pain and his body flipped through the air from the force of the punch. We rose to our feet. I reached for the atomizer, but I found out the left arm had tendon damage. I needed one hand to aim the thing and the other to work the pump, so that was out. I dove for the gun, bringing it up and firing. There had been too much warning for him, though, and he was already in bat form, too small and unpredictable to hit.

He swooped in, then, and turned human again at the last minute, punching me in the midsection. I grappled with him, grabbing him with my right hand, biting him and taking blood. It was horrible, but I could feel strength returning to my left hand. There was spite to me doing that, too, wanting him to feel a little of the pain he'd caused me. Then his hand closed on my throat, shutting off my windpipe. I wasn't sure what not being able to breathe would do to a vampire and I didn't really want to find out. It took awhile, but after we'd thrown a couple more punches at each other I could feel my muscles starting to protest.

Rasputin and I were getting closer to the railing as we fought, and I smiled inwardly. I was already dead, after all. If I could stop him, what happened to me wouldn't matter much. I'd read Sherlock Holmes and water had disabled Rasputin before. This would be my Reichenbach Falls, taking out a monster predator who would otherwise remain untouchable. I was literally already dead anyway, so I grappled him in a bear hug and leapt up and forward, taking us both over the side of the ship. I began to stab the lock pick into place, but even as I did, I found he was dissipating, turning into mist first and then a bat. Not good. I was plummeting toward the water of the harbor while Rasputin was flying away.

I didn't think I'd learn to fly on the way down this time, so I didn't even try turning into a bat. Instead, I spread out my limbs and shifted my weight, hoping to bring myself closer to the ship. I'd jumped too far and there was no way my trajectory was going to change enough, but then I remembered Cataracts' trick with her arms when she couldn't move her body. Sure enough, I could keep reaching out with my arms and finally sunk my nails into the metal, grabbing on. Of course, that didn't entirely halt my fall, as the rest of my body swung down. My right leg dipped into the water even as I brought the left up to brace against the hull. I took a deep breath and evaluated my situation.

First thing I did was scan overhead. I expected Rasputin to attack. He could fly effectively and had the advantage while I was clinging for safety.

There was no sign of him as far as I could see. The moonlight reflected off Yekaterina's red-gold hair, though, as she peered down at me. I appeared to be in no immediate danger and I began to pull myself up. My right leg was numb and I floundered as I tried to place it on the hull to climb. In fact, it was unresponsive to my attempts to move it from the knee down. I grumbled, and drew my arms back in, to normal length, bringing myself completely clear of the waterline in the process. Working my way up with only three functional limbs was tricky, but it was still easier for me to climb an extreme slope (about 110 degrees?) as a vampire than it would have been as a man. On the other hand, if I was still mortal, I could have managed the dive and swam to the dock. These thoughts passed through my head as I climbed.

Suddenly, the dark sky was sliced by a beam of light, bright enough to hurt my eyes when I looked at it. Even though it was dazzling, I thought I saw two tiny shapes silhouetted, back lit by it. The beam swept along, but didn't catch them. In fact, I realized that if I could see them, the person controlling the beam— and I was sure it was Clara— was in the wrong position to spot them. I was angry, not at her for missing them, but angry for her, that her courage and skill weren't enough, any more than mine had been. The bad guys were getting away, and we weren't going to be able to stop them.

The climb up seemed the longer for realizing that Rasputin and Yekaterina had left the ship. On the deck, I found my right leg had recovered enough to support my weight, and I limped down the gangplank to shore. The purser tried asking me a question, but I didn't really hear it. "Check with the other officers," I muttered. Everyone on the ship was likely to recover; that much I had for comfort.

A CONDITION

The spotlight still crossed the sky overhead, and it left enough of a trail of light I could follow it. Clara had to be there; I needed to make sure she and Eugene were all right, that the vampires hadn't managed to come after them in the end.

Passing by workers on the dock and the trickle of passengers still heading to ships left me feeling tense and shaky. I'd been through too much in one night. The light of their auras were like beacons, promising comfort, but I was getting better already at distancing myself from the vampire cravings. I kept my eyes on the sky and kept walking. Three parking lots over, I found them. It was some kind of VIP parking lot and my car was parked next to Eugene's. His had a dent in it. I had expected the battery to be hooked up to the searchlight, but instead, the searchlight was wired to a lamppost and the lamp was out, all juice being re-routed to the weaponized searchlight.

I hesitated. I wanted to go to them, but I was also scared to. I was ashamed and guilty that I hadn't managed to put an end to the two powerful vampires. I still needed to feed again, too. All that fighting and healing had left me craving blood and I could find some animals to drink from if I slunk off into the privacy of the nearby trees.

That's when Eugene shouted out, "Hey, Raf! Come on over. We have a couple of bottles for you! Nice, yummy blood!"

Clara's hand went to her forehead.

I came running, not for the bottles so much as to stop him shouting. On the other hand, it did solve the problem of how to finish healing up and stop the craving. Taking one from his hand, I said, "You didn't have to specify blood, you know. You could have just let anyone who overheard you think I'm a wino!"

"But then you might not know we had what you needed."

"How did you even get this? You didn't have time to go back to the lab."

"Medical offices at the port. There are some pretty nasty accidents on fishing boats. They try to have some emergency supplies on hand."

I drank the first bottle, then confessed. "Rasputin and Yekaterina... they got away. The light was a good idea, but they were tiny as bats. You didn't catch them. And I couldn't do enough."

Clara put her hand on my shoulder. "We saved more than a dozen lives tonight. We made sure the failure vampires wouldn't get loose in the city. We kept Eugene from being taken away to be their pet scientist. They've had to run. And we now know who and what we are looking for, thanks to your detective work. Missing a complete victory is not the same as having a complete defeat."

"We even have an idea of their eventual destination," I adjusted to this new line of thinking. "If they were travelling to France, they would have their valuables sent there, too. They won't want to lose that wealth, so you can have Interpol and the French police keep a watch on ports there."

"That's a good plan," Clara said. "I like a man who knows how to plan."

I started to smile. I took a half-step forward, thinking to kiss her and then I saw the pulse in her throat. I halted mid-step. "I love you, Clara. I can't believe how close we've become so fast, how well we work together. I wish things had gone differently, because I know you are the love of my life. But... my life is over. I'm undead. I may be different from other vampires, but I'm still way more like them than I ought to be. You aren't going to be safe with me. Not to mention, I obviously can't take a regular job."

She looked over at Eugene. "Give us a moment." She took hold of my arm and walked a short way away with me. "Rafael, you're absolutely right that you can't come to work as an Interpol officer in this state." Clara told me, "However, I want you to try to stop thinking of yourself as dead. I understand, this has changed you, but many things can change a person and sometimes they can change back. Try to think of yourself as having a condition."

"I'll try. But, Clara, the condition is contagious." I looked long and hard at her then added, "And you have no idea how much I want to give it to you."

Her lips pressed together, then she broke out in a laugh in spite of her attempt to stop it. "I rather think I do," she said. I was aghast a moment, and then I realized that 'give it to you' was often a euphemism for sex and didn't know whether to be embarrassed or just relieved that she could make a joke about it, but I laughed, too.

"That way, too," I admitted. "But seriously, suppressing the vampire takes work, and some things make it harder, like an injury or getting swept up in anger or desire. I need to practice. And I don't know if it will get easier or harder with time. I am sure, though, that I don't trust myself yet. If we're going to try to have a relationship, it's going to need to be long distance, at least until I know I won't be a danger to you."

"Well, I will have to do a lot of travel, anyhow, to get the team started on finding a cure."

"Wait. The team?" I gave her a speculative look. "Is Witch-Hunters still operational?"

"It's hard to say."

"Well, they are or they aren't."

"Secrecy spells make things hard to say," she emphasized the last three words.

"But why—"

"We are officially not operational. It was a wartime project. We are no longer fighting a war."

"But if occult stuff is real— and we know it is— it's not going to go away, and the need to know about it doesn't go away, just because the Nazis have been stopped."

"Exactly. Which is why we're being funded off the books. A little bit private funding, a little bit of diverted funds. And generally doing day jobs."

"Interpol is your *day job*?"

"The spooks come out at night. We'll get some of our best people researching your condition. I'm not even sure you're really undead, Raf. You weren't bothered by holy symbols, and you... you do have a gift for healing."

"I am a vampire, though. The ocean left my leg dead for minutes."

"Ocean. What were you doing in the—" she stopped herself before getting derailed completely. "We'll get into that in the full debriefing. We don't know exactly what's happening with you, and I'm not giving up on you. We will find some way to help you."

"You really think we can be together again someday?"

"I'm sure of it."

"I like the way you think." After so many times I'd had my heart broken, it was boggling my mind that this one time where breaking up with me was probably the only sensible thing to do was the one time I'd found someone who wouldn't let go. I stayed focused on her lips this time, as I leaned forward and kissed her.

There was a whistle and some applause. I looked over to see Eugene grinning at us. "Are you about done with your private conference? For those of us not keeping warm canoodling, it's getting a bit chilly out here."

I drove us to his place in my car. The dent in

his was caused by nothing more serious than his own tendency to get distracted while driving; usually he had a chauffeur, but the vampires hadn't wanted anyone who might have questions. Here I was, back with normal people doing normal things. The monster wasn't under the bed, he was being asked to come up and have a scotch and soda and fill everyone in on the details.

The drink was good, though. Apparently, I could still enjoy imbibing, even if I couldn't eat. It took the edge off. The first thing to straighten out was to try to set Eugene right about Katie not being real, just an alias of a vampiress who was trying to use his genius to make them more invulnerable. I had to tell him that Tammy had been killed, which was hard news for both of us and I think helped him take the Katie thing more seriously. Irene at least would recover and probably be happy to come back to her old job.

Eugene insisted on paying me, not only for the job he'd asked me to do but also my follow-up on the vampires. Getting paid for rescuing him made sense to me, but I tried to put up an argument about the time I'd spent lying in the morgue in between. His point that I wouldn't have been there if it hadn't been for his job made sense, and I gave in. More than that, Eugene wanted to be part of my recovery team, and do whatever else he could to help me cope with what had been done to me. The legal term for it is "to make whole".

I figured for the time being, I could probably do with blood drained at the butchers' shops, but Eugene could get some from laboratory suppliers in case that didn't work out. He also threatened— well, promised, I just had some quiet qualms about it— to send a designer to my office and apartment to plan to modify the lighting, particularly excluding sunlight, and make any other adjustments I might think of to fit my new lifestyle. Most of all, though he wanted to work on making a new generation of anti-vampire technology based on our experiences so far.

Eugene might have reacted to my story by taking an interest in improving our arsenal, but Clara was listening to what I was conveying about everyone's behavior.

"It sounds like Yekaterina is the more intelligent of the two."

"He's definitely the leader," I argued.

"That doesn't matter." Clara said. "Leaders are often simply the people who expect to lead. He likely is a megalomaniac. Yekaterina, though, she sounds subtle. She's the sort to get someone to do what she wants by making them think it's their own idea."

I was about to argue that, but it occurred to me that Yekaterina had been the source of my information that I could only escape becoming a vampire if he died before me. "Maybe. And she certainly knows how to play two sides at once."

Clara looked at me steadily. "She may be the more dangerous one as far as you're concerned."

"You hardly know her. You haven't even spoken to each other."

"I know she wrapped Eugene around her little finger in no time and that you feel ambiguously sympathetic to her."

"Is it that obvious?"

"You're a kind man, Rafael. You'll have to work not to have your kindness used against you."

I thought about it. "I'll keep on guard around her if and when I am dealing with her again, and any strategies I come up with won't assume she's going to be any less aggressive to others than Rasputin is. Like with any other person engaged in conspiracy and murder. But I'm not going to stop being kind. Kindness is important. We must never forget that, or we can become what we fight." I wasn't just thinking about the vampires. Everyone makes dozens, maybe hundreds of choices every day. We can be kind, try to help people, try to understand them, and be a friend even to strangers. Or we can harden ourselves and leave everyone to look after their own interests. From what I'd seen, hardened societies destroy their own.

"We'd never ask that," said Eugene. And that's why he's my friend, no matter how different we are. We both believe in kindness.

I went back to telling the story and when I came to the bit where I threw both of us over the rail, Clara interrupted again. "Are you crazy? I told you how dangerous running water would be."

"Yeah. And I wanted to stop Rasputin. I thought it was my best play."

"Is that all?"

"I want to live, Clara. I do. But I already died, and I do not know how to be what I am. If it had worked, it would have been worth it. But as soon as I realized it didn't work, I saved myself. Now it's time for me to work on coping with what I am. I've got plenty of reasons to stick around." I gave her hand a squeeze. She was plenty kind herself.

Around two in the morning, Clara went to a guest room. It had been a long day for her. Eugene was still going, sketching ideas. Katie might have been subtly switching him to a night schedule, but he'd always been more driven by the inner workings of his brain than by the clock. I wasn't the least bit sleepy, having been in the big sleep for a few days. About a half hour before dawn, though, drowsiness hit me like a wave ready to drag me under. I fought it. I needed to know if I could function by day. Not being able to go out in the light was bad enough, but to keep my business, I had to at least be able to make phone calls, things like that. And I needed my work right now. It gave a sense of stability to my new existence.

When I got hold of Flannery, I found out it had taken him two days to get a search warrant, and that had been long enough. When he'd gotten to The Silver Samovar, they found the proprietor's body hanging from the rafters. Adrian Petrov's death had been chalked up to a suicide, maybe because of the potential legal trouble. Flannery had asked the coroner about the possibility of homicide, but the weight of the body had definitely fallen rather than been hoisted into place, and even Moose wasn't strong enough to have lifted the man into a noose, struggling or unconscious. There was no sign of any jewelry, except for the three pieces I'd hidden, exactly where I cached them. After a few pleasantries, I said goodbye to him.

Clara was just getting up and making coffee, so I told her we'd want more prints from the photographs of the jewelry from The Silver Samovar. More than likely, once Rasputin and Yekaterina decided to move on, they wanted to get what they could of their resources back. Rather than settle for what they could find of what they sold the first time, they took the lot. If they sold it again, that could give us another way to get a line on them.

After checking in with my messenger service, I finally couldn't think of any reason to continue postponing sleep that didn't involve being afraid of what I might dream or how I might wake up, so I took over the guest room. It was on the interior, so I didn't have to worry about sunlight, and the scent of Clara's hair lingering on the pillows was a bonus.

Maybe that's why I had no nightmares. Maybe I just sleep like the dead. Either way, at sunset I was awake again and had no memory of dreams or sensations in the time that passed between. The hunger wasn't too bad, either, though I made sure to have a pint before meeting up with anyone. Why make it harder for myself?

Clara was going to take a morning flight to France to set things up there to prepare the local police as best she could for Rasputin and Yekaterina. She was also going to meet with her other team, so there would be people who were properly ready for the situation. I told her to change it for an evening plane so I could go with her.

Eugene looked alarmed. "You can't do that!" he warned me. "The plane travels too high in the atmosphere. A delay in the flight, getting rerouted, if anything goes wrong, you'll be close to the sun without so much of a buffer between, and then..." He made noises and hand gestures indicating sizzling, bursting into flame, exploding, and drifting down into a pile of ashes. I doubted ashes would really make a musical tinkling sound but I didn't critique the logic on that.

"Thanks for that vivid depiction of my potential demise."

"You're welcome. I thought you might not be aware of the danger."

Clara brought up something else. "Actually, Raf, I told Sir Lynn— the head of our little band— that you would probably want to come. He said that we don't really know that the vampires got on another ship going the same way instead of doubling back. They might be waiting until we clear out to have another go at Eugene."

I frowned. I wanted to refute it, but I couldn't. It would have been a good move. "So I stick to New York until they make a move or you find evidence of them elsewhere?"

"It seems smart to me," said Eugene, who was doing some calculations on paper while talking. "After all, you'll need to explain to Katie about her evil twin whenever we find her."

I exchanged looks with Clara. "You're right. He absolutely needs protection."

Later that evening we went up to the observation deck. Clara figured if she was going to ask me to protect myself and keep sane while we sought a way to restore me, she should set me an example and face her own fears. When we got there, she stood by my side, near the edge, overlooking the city. "It is beautiful up here. Like looking down at the stars."

"It's a beautiful world. This just gives us a new perspective."

She put her hand to my cheek. "There's so much out there. As large as this view is, it's just one."

"A world that has things I never dreamed existed."

"But the most important things are still the same."

I'll spare you further details. Our second date may not have been as physically intimate as the first, but we were emotionally closer than ever. Parting was hard, but it was best to keep the relationship long distance for now. Eugene was going to be working with me locally and keeping in touch with the magical experts at WITCH Hunters to fix me up. Clara had my phone numbers, office and house, and Eugene's as well since I was going to be spending a lot of time there. I also had a plan to take Eugene's mind off Katie— I'd let Pearl know he'd been tricked. She might be old enough to be his mother but they had an on and off affair going and she'd keep him busy for a while.

And me? I had my work, and when things were slow, I had a brand new set of abilities to explore. I wasn't done dealing with the dead yet, either. My next major case involved a ghost... but that's a different story.

EPILOGUE: PUTTING THE FUN IN FUNERAL

"Good news," Eugene told me. "I've managed to find a heartbeat of a sort. It's about five beats per minute when you're resting."

"Of a sort?"

"The pumping action has a different kind of sound to it. There's kind of a sloshing, sucking noise. You mentioned vampire blood is thicker, right? Still, it had to be there, or destroying the heart wouldn't be so useful in dealing with a vampire. I'd like to scan your internal organs. What do you think of ultrasound?"

"Based on prior experience, incredibly painful."

"That doohickey was supposed to be irritating. I'll try and make a scanner you find soothing. It's got to be safer than doing an X-ray. There's a real chance that could set you on fire."

"Is this stuff really going to help find a way to give me my life back?"

Eugene put his hand on my shoulder. "I'm not

going to promise you that. But I'm not going to tell you it's not worth trying. There weren't treatments for any medical condition until researchers worked on it and finally there were. You've got a functioning body, so by some measure, indeed, by any scientific measure, you are alive. On the other hand, you did die, although according to your body temperature, it was within the last half hour, so... who do you want invited to your funeral?"

"What?"

"I was thinking the Saturday after next would be a good day to throw your funeral, but if you need more time to get your family or Army buddies or exes here, we can always put it off. It's not like the body is going to decay."

"Eugene, we're not going to have a funeral for me."

"We're not going to bury you, of course, but dying's a major life event. What kind of a friend would I be if I didn't offer to host a nice funeral?"

"A discreet one."

"You don't want this to be made a big deal of?"

"Of course not. Tell me you didn't notify my parents of my death?"

"Not yet. I was thinking engraved invitations, black borders, very tasteful."

I put my face in my hands a minute to get my

thoughts together so I could explain things properly. "Eugene. I want my existence to continue as normally as possible. And integral to that plan is for people not to think I am dead or a walking undead monster. As far as anyone outside of you, me, Clara, and any experts she deems need to know, I am still just a plain old detective making a living."

"There was going to be a New Orleans jazz funeral band."

I hesitated before shaking my head. "How about we just go out to a bar for a few drinks? There's a little blues band that plays on Fridays at Treacle Tap on 128th St. There's a waitress there who could be Josephine Baker's twin. We'll have just as much fun and not make either of my parents pass out."

"Should I cancel the lilies?"

"Change it to roses for Clara."

"Fine. What about your casket?"

"You didn't order me a casket, did you, Eugene?" He bit his lip. "Eugene, cancel the casket. I am NOT going to sleep in a casket!"

ABOUT THE AUTHOR

Helen Krummenacker is uncomfortable talking about herself in the third person, so I won't. I helped create the Para-Earth Series by Allan Krummenacker and Helen Krummenacker. I have a B.S. in Mathematics, and hope that writing proofs has helped keep my fiction streamlined and avoid plot holes. Hobbies include gaming (tabletop/roleplaying), dancing, and painting. Health issues limit my activity level, but I manage to work as an accounting technician by day and escape into mystery and adventure genres at night. I'm allergic to garlic and sunlight, but I promise I don't thirst for blood, just coffee and maybe a bit of bourbon.

Other books I have worked on are: The Bridge, The Ship, The Vampyre Blogs: Coming Home, and The Vampyre Blogs: One Day at a Time.

38235996R00133

Made in the USA
San Bernardino, CA
09 June 2019